D1532351

ISLAND SOJOURN

Other books by Katrina Thomas:

Father of Convenience
Everything Wright

ISLAND SOJOURN

•

Katrina Thomas

AVALON BOOKS
NEW YORK

0 2 2 3 1 0

F
Tho

Published by Thomas Bouregy & Co., Inc.
160 Madison Avenue, New York, NY 10016

Library of Congress Cataloging-in-Publication Data

Thomas, Katrina, 1959–
    Island sojourn / Katrina Thomas.
        p. cm.
    ISBN 978-0-8034-7755-1 (hardcover : acid-free paper)
1. Women fire fighters—Fiction.   2. Sisters—Fiction.
3. Mate selection—Fiction.   4. Hatteras Island (N.C.)—
Fiction.   I. Title.
    PS3620.H629I75 2010
    813'.6—dc22

                                        2009045279

PRINTED IN THE UNITED STATES OF AMERICA
ON ACID-FREE PAPER
BY HADDON CRAFTSMEN, BLOOMSBURG, PENNSYLVANIA

For the "Monnat Sisterhood"
My grandmother Catherine and her daughters
My mother, Rosemary, and my aunts Edna,
Ellen, Elizabeth, and Patricia
Their legacy of hard work and perseverance
will continue to guide future generations
of the Monnat family.

Chapter One

"We've got to get out of here!"

Delaney Sutton felt a tug on her elbow as a rumbling and then a crash from above her head filled her ears. Nausea twisted in her stomach while fellow firefighters rushed past her in the dim corridor of the abandoned warehouse.

"That sounds like another support beam giving way. Come on, Delaney!"

Beneath her bulky uniform and heavy gear, her arms broke out in a cold sweat. Her throat constricted; and her hands, covered by stiff gloves, began to shake.

Someone pushed her toward the narrow, enclosed staircase leading to the ground floor of the building. Her boots weighed her down like lead as she stumbled on the top step. Grasping for the railing, she regained her

1

balance and hurried on unsteady legs to the bottom of the stairs.

Once outdoors, in the bright summer heat, she removed her helmet and yanked off her mask. She gulped in air and willed her heart to resume its normal rhythm.

Her fingers trembled as she took off her gloves, unfastened her uniform coat, and peeled it away from her perspiration-drenched company shirt. She forced a smile as an emergency medical technician urged her to take a seat on the tailgate of a nearby ambulance and secured a blood pressure cuff around her upper left arm.

"How is she?"

Delaney looked up to see Chief Adler striding toward the rig. She winced at the tone of his gruff, impatient voice.

He pointed a gloved finger at her. "I want to see you in my office as soon as we're back in quarters, Sutton."

Less than an hour later, Delaney entered the company's firehouse and walked to the chief's office as her stomach twisted in knots. While she considered whether or not to knock on the open door, Chief Richard Adler raised his head and waved her in with a big hand and thick, stubby fingers.

"Come in, Sutton, and have a seat."

"You wanted to see me, Chief?"

The metal chair squeaked as the tall man with a sandy blond crew cut leaned back in it and leveled his blue eyes on Delaney. She held her breath.

"What happened in that warehouse today? Petersen said you hesitated up there."

She swallowed and looked away from him. Shifting in her seat, she fingered the gloves in her hand.

"What's going on with you lately?"

Her eyes darted back to him. "Nothing, Chief."

"Is there anything you want to tell me?"

She shook her head. "I guess I lost my bearings for a second. That's all."

"Are you sure that's it? You haven't been yourself these past few weeks. Petersen and Conrad have both commented on the change in you."

"Change, Chief?"

"You've become quiet and withdrawn. We've all noticed it."

She pushed a strand of hair behind her ear. "Just because I don't hoot and holler over some stupid game on television or laugh at the guys' tasteless jokes doesn't mean something's wrong."

Chief Adler leaned toward her and set his elbows on his desk. "You used to be the one telling those tasteless jokes." He studied her for a long moment. "Listen, Delaney, I know you took Hal Barker's death really hard after that explosion. It's been less than eight months since you've been back from medical leave."

She opened her mouth to speak, but he held up his hand to stop her. She blew out a puff of air as he continued. "You passed the medical, and Psych cleared you to return to duty so I know you can do the work, but what I need to know is if you *want* to be here."

She almost rose from her chair. "Of course, I want to be here. I've wanted to be a firefighter since I was six years old. This is my life's dream."

"Dreams change. People change. I want you to take some time off to think about what you want to do with the rest of your life."

"I don't need to take time to think."

"Listen, Delaney, you're like a daughter to me. You've been pushing yourself too hard, working overtime, and volunteering to take double shifts. I don't want to see you burn out at twenty-six."

"I'm not going to burn out."

"Not if I can help it." He stood up from his chair and rounded the desk to stand next to her. "You need a break. Except for that six-month medical leave, you haven't taken more than two days off at a time in over five years. I want you to use your four weeks of accrued leave to get away from the job. Get out of Richmond. Take a trip. Go someplace relaxing."

"But I don't want to take time off."

"This is not a request, Sutton. As of this minute, you're on a mandated vacation."

The sound of an unfamiliar voice right outside her bedroom door interrupted the same dream Delaney had been having for months. In a semiconscious state, she rolled from one side of the twin bed to the other. Keeping her eyes closed, she tucked the pillow in the crook of her arm and pulled the sheet and blanket up to her chin.

Brr! How could it be so cold in North Carolina in July? Someone must have lowered the temperature of the air conditioning unit.

She considered dragging herself from the warmth of the bed to get another blanket from the closet, but she was so tired. It could not be more than six o'clock, and she and Cassie had stayed up talking until after three.

She opened one eye and tried to focus on the other twin bed in the dim light. Empty. Of course. As always, Cassie was up and energetic and cheerful before the day had barely started.

Delaney groaned and pulled the pillow over her head as her thoughts drifted to the telephone conversation she'd had with her sister earlier that week, right after Chief Adler had put her on vacation for a month. Depression and disillusionment had threatened to cloud her thoughts, and she'd needed the comfort of a familiar voice and a sympathetic ear.

"Vacation! That's perfect, Del. Now you won't have to hurry back after the Sutton Sisterhood Sojourn."

"I can't believe you still want to do that weekend retreat. I thought after you got married, the Sutton sisters would put the old tradition to rest."

"Are you kidding? It's the best relaxation time we have all year. The Sojourn is our chance to relax, rejuvenate, and reconnect with each other. Come on, Del, you've got no excuse. You can lounge at the beach for a month."

"I thought I'd just stay here in Richmond."

"All alone in that tiny apartment? What kind of vacation is that?"

"I'm not alone. I have Max."

"Max is a cat. You need people. Del, you need your sisters." Cassandra Sutton Maguire sighed over the telephone line. "You have to join us. The Sutton Sisterhood is just not complete without you."

"Well—"

"Say yes. Bri and Allison have left already. They wanted to get the beach house opened up and make sure everything was set for the weekend. I'm leaving Raleigh tomorrow afternoon. Say you'll come and stay. Please, please, *please?*"

At that moment, the memory of Cassie's voice on the phone mingled with the quiet baritone one Delaney thought she had imagined in the hall outside the bedroom. The masculine sound interrupted her recollection of the conversation with her sister. She pulled the pillow from her ears and listened with concentrated effort.

A man? In the Sutton beach house at dawn? This was the Sisterhood weekend. No men were allowed.

"It just quit yesterday. We can't wash any clothes." Cassie's voice.

But that wasn't Tim Maguire's voice giving the low, smooth reply. Not only was it not Cassie's husband of one month, but it also wasn't Brianna's Will, or Allison's Zack, or their father. Delaney was sure she did not recognize that voice.

Max stretched to his full thirty-six inches beside Delaney and meowed his protest as she brushed him with the edge of the pillow case. Still listening, she tossed the pillow toward the foot of the bed and rubbed the feline's stomach in apology.

"Sorry, Max. I wonder who's the man with the gorgeous sounding voice."

The cat grumbled his reply in a language Delaney had not been able to decipher in the five years he'd been her roommate. She continued to rub under his chin as the unfamiliar male spoke again.

"It spun out for one load, but not for the next?"

Delaney listened to metal clanking against metal and scooped the cat up into her arms. "Come on, Max. We need to take a look."

In her wide-legged flannel pajama bottoms and faded Virginia Commonwealth University tee shirt, she set her bare feet onto the floor. With quiet steps, she padded to the door.

The small laundry area, hidden when not in use by varnished louvered doors, was located right across the hall from the beach house bedroom she had always shared with Cassie. Opening the door, she peeked out of the four-inch slit and gazed appreciatively at the appealing back view of a tall man who was bending over the washing machine.

"Mmm. Nice."

Max responded to her whispered remark by eying the stranger with suspicion and flicking his tail in slow, precise movements. A rumble of discontent rolled from somewhere inside the cat.

"Hush." Delaney moved her hand from the door and bent to rub the cat's chin, but the door suddenly swung open and hit the wall with a bang.

The man rose and turned with a surprised look on his face. Thick dark hair. Expressive blue eyes. High, tanned cheekbones. Thin nose. Kissable mouth.

Kissable mouth? . . . Wow! Where's that coming from? Delaney stopped her mental assessment of the stranger smiling at her.

"Well, hi. I hope I didn't wake you."

Wake me? She brushed messy blond waves from her face and stared at Gareth.

That was his name. Gareth. At least, that was the name embroidered in dark gray thread on the patch above the left shirt pocket of his gray uniform. Gareth.

"No, you didn't wake . . . Oh, I'm not dressed. I'm sorry!" She clutched Max and slammed the door in the handsome stranger's face.

Jumping back into bed, she dragged the sheet and blanket over her head and groaned into the muffled darkness. Max wriggled in protest and pawed at the material confining him. Delaney lifted a corner and released the poor feline, who jumped to her sister's bed in one graceful leap and settled onto the pillow where he proceeded to wash himself and send Delaney indignant glares with his blue-green eyes.

Under the blankets and feeling completely humiliated that a stranger named Gareth had seen her in old pajamas with her hair tangled and a mouthy cat in her arms, Delaney lay awake for a long time listening to the stranger clanging and moving around outside the closed door. After a while, her heart stopped racing, and she began to doze again.

As she drifted off the sleep, she dreamed, as usual, of firefighting and rescuing people. She climbed ladders and broke down doors. She pulled victims from smoke-filled rooms. She rescued dogs and cats and exotic birds and presented them to their anxious and relieved owners who smiled their gratitude with teary eyes.

While she slept, she assisted other firefighters. She warned them of collapsing ceilings and alternate exits. She searched for coworkers disoriented and wandering in dark, unfamiliar structures. She dragged fellow fire-fighters, knocked unconscious from explosions, away from danger.

Delaney's dreams were always similar. She did her job. She followed protocol and used her skills to save people and property.

The only difference in her typical dream this time was the face of the victim staring back at her. When she leaned over to lift the mask of the fallen firefighter, she did not see an unrecognizable, nebulous form. This time, she saw Gareth, the stranger repairing the washer. As she pulled the head gear and breathing apparatus from him, his expressive blue eyes and very appealing mouth smiled up at her.

When Delaney awoke again, she couldn't remember how many times she had rescued Gareth and then stared back into his handsome face. The dream had been like a television rerun that looped and looped and refused to stop airing in her head.

Bright summer sunlight spilled around the edges of the room—darkening shade on the windows when she finally sat up and threw her blankets toward the foot of the bed. Max, lying beside her again, protested the sudden movements with a loud meow and jumped onto the floor. He sauntered toward the closed door and looked back at her with an impatient stare.

"I'm coming. I'm coming."

She took a moment to stretch and then reached for the doorknob. Cautiously, she opened the door a crack and peered into the hallway. The louvered doors of the laundry room were open, and the dryer hummed, but the area was deserted. No Gareth. No sisters. Only a load of laundry tumbling and fluffing in the dryer.

Delaney swung the door open all the way, and Max bolted out and scurried down the hall of the third floor of the beach house toward the stairs leading to the second floor. Delaney followed as she passed through the large, empty family room. From there, she headed to the spacious kitchen and breakfast nook. Pulling open a sliding glass door, she stepped out onto the second-story balcony, which looked out over white sand dunes and the beach beyond.

On white wicker chairs around a matching wicker

table sat her three older sisters: Allison Sutton Cabot, Brianna Sutton Sears, and Cassandra Sutton Maguire. Like Delaney, all of them were blond and petite with gray eyes and fair skin. Their laughter over a joke one of them had just told floated to her ears as she approached the group.

Three pairs of smiling eyes turned to look at her and then wide grins spread across their faces. They all jumped up from their seats at once and rushed to greet her with hugs and kisses.

"You're awake!"

"We didn't think you were ever getting up, Delaney."

"You don't plan to sleep away your entire vacation, do you, Del?"

Delaney used a hand to shade her eyes from the brilliant North Carolina sun that radiated heat with fierce intensity onto the open balcony. "What time is it?"

"Almost eleven." Cassie, the sister next to her in birth line and the one who had kept Delaney up until three talking about her incredible husband of one month and the joys of marital bliss, stroked Max's fur as he curled on her lap and gave Delaney a smug feline look. "We thought we would have to start banging on something nice and loud to get you to roll out of bed before lunchtime."

Delaney slid into an empty chair at the table. Pulling toward her a pitcher of orange juice with lemon, lime, and orange slices floating in it, she poured herself a glass. She took a long drink of the refreshing pulpy liquid and then leaned back in her seat. "Somebody already did that." She glanced at Max soaking in Cassie's attention as her sister rubbed the spot behind his ears that he liked so much. He yawned and snuggled against Cassie's cotton swimsuit cover-up while looking back at Delaney out of the corners of his sleepy eyes. "Max and I were rudely interrupted by a stranger clanging on the washing machine."

Allison nodded. "I had to call a plumber."

"The last load didn't spin out well yesterday," Brianna explained as she shifted in her chair and smoothed her hands over her swollen abdomen.

Delaney scowled. "We could have gone to a laundromat. I came for peace and quiet, not to listen to noisy wrenches slamming against metal pipes." *Or to see a handsome plumber whose distracting image transplanted itself right in the middle of my dreams.*

Cassie rolled her eyes. "He wasn't that loud. In fact, I mentioned to him that you were still sleeping when I showed him to the laundry room."

"He was so polite," Brianna said.

"And very handsome," Allison added.

Cassie nodded. "With the cutest butt—aside from Tim's, of course."

Delaney stared at her. "You just got married."

Cassie grinned. "I can still enjoy a nice back view, can't I?"

Allison reached for the pitcher and refilled her glass of juice. "Enough about the plumber. We have more important issues to discuss. Let's not forget our purpose for being here this weekend."

Cassie cleared her throat. "Our purpose is to relax, rejuvenate, reconnect with our common heritage, and solidify our sibling bonds."

"The annual Sutton Sisterhood Sojourn has officially begun." Brianna stretched out her legs and kicked off her fluorescent pink flip flops. "What's the plan this year?"

"Plan?" Delaney groaned. "Can't we just have a quiet, enjoyable weekend together without some complicated, preconceived program of events?"

All three of her sisters stared at her and shouted "No!" in unison. Max meowed his disapproval of the loud, unexpected disturbance.

Delaney shook her head and threw her arms in the air. "Okay, I'll try to listen with an open mind, but I'm not dressing up in tights and a tutu like I did for Brianna's ballet bash four years ago. I look horrible in pink."

Brianna wiggled her toes. "You were adorable in that outfit. I still have the video we made that night. It must be around here somewhere."

Delaney groaned again and covered her face with her hands. "You swore you'd destroy that tape."

"How about a carnival theme this year?" Cassie smoothed the fur on Max's back. "Del could dress up as a clown. I think she'd film really well with orange and purple hair and a big red sponge nose."

Delaney wadded a beach towel hanging over one of the wicker chairs and tossed it at her newlywed sister.

Max grumbled in protest when the thick terry cloth thudded against him.

Delaney squinted. "Sorry, Max, but Cassie deserved that. I'm not going to make a fool of myself this weekend. I'm twenty-six years old now, and I no longer want to be the brunt of my older sisters' relentless attempts to humiliate me."

She glanced around the table at each of the blond women sitting there. "Come on. Haven't I earned the right to be treated like an adult, like the rest of the Sutton sisters?"

"An adult?" Brianna wrapped her arms around her stomach and smiled sweetly at Delaney. "You'll always be our little sister. In our eyes, you'll never really be all grown up."

Allison held up her hand. "But Delaney does bring up an interesting point."

She narrowed her eyes at the eldest Sutton sibling— the quiet, nurturing, but always scheming, leader of the group. "What point is that, exactly?"

Allison combed the fingers of both hands through her short hair and sighed. "The fact that you turned twenty-six in the spring."

"So?"

"So, you're not getting any younger," Brianna said.

"You'll be thirty before you know it," Cassie added.

"We're worried about you, Delaney. You have dark circles under your eyes. Your face looks tired." With a sincere expression of concern on her face, Allison studied her. "You look like you haven't been taking care of yourself."

Delaney shook her head. "What does any of this have to do with your efforts to always make me look ridiculous at these Sisterhood Sojourns? How many years have we been meeting here on Hatteras Island on this same weekend in July? Let's see." She did a mental calculation. "Since I was twelve, so that makes it fourteen years. Fourteen years of humiliation. For over a decade, I've been forced to endure the outlandish roles you, my so-called loving sisters, have devised to make me look stupid."

"Oh, be honest." Brianna shooed away a dragonfly that was flitting around her hand. "It hasn't been that bad. Didn't you have a good time wearing the plaid kilt and matching hat with the little ball on top?"

Delaney rolled her eyes. "The kilt I almost threw up on after eating that Scottish dish of animal parts that should never be consumed by human beings?"

Cassie touched Brianna's arm. "And that sweet little elf suit with the green tights and slippers with bells on the toes. Did Del look cute in that outfit, or what?"

Everyone but Delaney smiled at the memories of past Sutton sister get-togethers and nodded. She rolled her eyes and finished her juice.

Allison reached over and squeezed Delaney's shoulders. "I think you'll be happy to learn that I've been considering some interesting variations for this year's weekend. I think I have the perfect plan."

Delaney had no desire to find out what mortification her eldest sibling had envisioned for her. She reached for a purple plum from the dish to her right. "Let's get the suspense over with. I can't wait to hear."

Allison inhaled a long, dramatic breath and picked up a floppy straw beach hat from a nearby chair. "I've selected four distinct themes, one for each evening."

She dropped folded yellow papers in the hat. "The cards indicate the theme for each evening and your night for preparing, shopping, creating costumes, cooking, and doing anything else you decide to do for your theme. The festivities will begin at six each evening, starting tonight."

Allison smiled as she looked around the table. "How simple or complicated you make it is up to you. You can have a classy, elegant evening, or a silly, unusual one. The choice is yours. The only rule is that all the materials and ingredients you use have to be from the beach house or bought somewhere here on the island." She settled her gaze on Delaney. "You get to choose first, since you think we've treated you unfairly in the past."

Delaney was already suspicious. "Are we revealing the theme we choose with the others before our assigned evening?"

Allison shook her head. "I'm the only one who knows all the themes, but I won't know which one each of you chooses. It's your choice if your want to tell anyone else."

Delaney narrowed her eyes at the eldest Sutton. "What's the catch?"

Her sister appeared completely innocent. Delaney studied Brianna and Cassie in turn to discover a hint of the secret they shared, but she saw nothing beyond guilt-free expressions.

"So, I can make any one of you wear dumb costumes and do foolish things as long as everything I request relates to the theme I choose from the hat?"

Allison nodded with a solemn expression. Brianna raised her eyebrows.

Cassie shrugged and smoothed Max's back with her hand. "Sounds good to me, Del. Let's pick."

With dubious caution, Delaney swept her gaze around the table at her sisters once again and then sighed. "Okay, I'll play your game—but I refuse to wear a tutu."

With a smile Delaney did not trust, Allison shook the straw hat to mix up the yellow cards.

Delaney inhaled a deep breath and closed her eyes. She chose a folded slip of paper and hid it in her palm as she read it, although she had serious doubts that the others were not already aware of the theme in the hat.

Hawaiian luau. Friday. The theme had potential.

Her mind raced with prospects. *Colorful skirts. Hulas. Flower leis. Drinks with umbrellas.*

"I have to be ready by tonight? That doesn't give me much time."

"I'll help you, Del." Cassie offered as she stuck her hand into the hat.

"Right, so you can spy on everything I have planned and snitch to the others. No thanks."

Delaney tucked the paper in the pocket of her flannel pajama bottoms. Yes, she could put together a nice Hawaiian luau and maybe make her sisters feel just a little embarrassed in the process.

Cassie, Brianna, and Allison chose in birth order from youngest to oldest. To Delaney's surprise, none of her sisters gave a single clue of the theme on the paper she had chosen. In fact, they were unusually quiet. She took one final look around the table to catch a glimpse of any underhandedness that might be occurring, but found none.

"So, we're all set? Everyone knows her assignment?" Allison spoke in her best teacher voice.

Feeling like a sixth grader again, Delaney joined the others in a chorus of "Yes, Mrs. Cabot." Even on summer vacation, her oldest sister did not stray far from her chosen profession.

"Great, because I'm hungry." Allison rose from her seat.

Brianna stood and rubbed her lower back. "It's time for lunch."

"Let's eat out," Allison said.

Cassie grinned. "I suggest the Nautical Nymph."

"That sounds good. We'll leave in fifteen minutes." Allison turned to Delaney. "Can you be ready by then?"

Delaney grinned as she stood. "I'll be ready before

any of the rest of you. I'm used to getting dressed
quickly. I'm a firefighter, remember?"

Stalks of sea oats waved on the dunes as Delaney
gazed out one of the side windows of Allison's sport util-
ity vehicle. As usual, she and Cassie were relegated to
the back while the two older sisters sat in the front seat as
they sped south along North Carolina Route 12 from
Avon to Buxton.

For reasons she couldn't understand, Delaney's mind
drifted to the tall, intriguing stranger who had been at
her parents' beach house earlier that morning repairing
the washing machine. Gareth.

His first name. That was all she knew about him.
Well, she did know a few things. He had gorgeous sap-
phire blue eyes, a mouth that could probably kiss away
any troubled thought, and a lean, muscular body that
made her heart jump when she looked at him. Other
than physical appearance, though, she knew very little
about Gareth the plumber.

No man had ever invaded her dreams like Gareth. Before, the face behind the mask had always been formless
and without distinction. She had never recognized the
fallen firefighter. Frustration often plagued her when
she awoke because she'd failed to identify the man she
had rescued, but now he had a face. Gareth's face.

She was just being fanciful, she knew. She was al-
lowing her mind to wander to silly, whimsical places

where she did not want to go. She was on Hatteras Island for a rest, not for dating and romance.

"Isn't that the plumber who fixed the washer, Allie?"

Delaney dragged her mind from her fanciful thoughts and turned to look in the direction Brianna was pointing as they pulled into the parking area of the Nautical Nymph Inn. Was she talking about the man in the khaki pants and navy polo shirt walking next to that willowy brunette? The couple leaving the restaurant?

"It looks just like him," Cassie said as she reached for her purse and opened the right back door of the SUV. "Who do you think he's with?"

Delaney did not want to know. She wanted to hide in the back seat of her sister's car until he had driven away in his. She had showered and dressed and styled her hair since he had last seen her, but etched in her mind forever was the way she imagined she had appeared to him earlier that morning when she'd rolled out of bed and opened the door to look right into the fantastic blue eyes of Gareth the plumber.

She hunched her shoulders and melted into the soft leather seat of the vehicle. She really wasn't that hungry anyway.

"Hurry up, Del!"

"Let's go. I'm eating for two, and this baby wants lunch."

Releasing a sigh and keeping her head bent, Delaney crawled from the car and scooted to Allison's left, where she hoped she would blend in with the other

Suttons as Gareth and his companion walked past them.

He was not wearing his crisp gray uniform, but she would have recognized that handsome face anywhere. From the corner of her eyes, she appraised his toned body and long legs. He wore khakis even better than he did the uniform. *Incredible!*

"Good afternoon, ladies." He flashed white teeth, and the warmth in his smile made his blue eyes dance. To Delaney's surprise, he gave a set of keys to the woman, who continued to walk away from them, and he approached the Sutton sisters. "How's the washer doing?"

Allison returned his smile. "Fine. We did one load, like you told us to do."

He nodded. "Remember, the repairs I made were just temporary. I ordered the part you need—but, unfortunately, it has to come from Kitty Hawk. The delivery van should get down here sometime this afternoon."

"Thank you so much." Allison stepped behind Delaney and nudged her toward him. "You know all of us but our youngest sister, Delaney."

She stumbled forward and stared into sparkling blue eyes that seemed to be laughing at her. The recognition she saw in them made her want to crawl right into nearby Pamlico Sound and swim until she reached the North Carolina mainland.

"It's nice to meet you, Delaney." He held out his right hand to her. "Gareth Collins."

His handshake was firm, and the warm, rough skin

of his fingers reminded her of sand on a sunny day. Sensations she neither wanted nor could explain rushed through her and made her legs weak. When she tried to inhale a breath to steady her nerves, her head filled with the subtle scents of fresh shower gel and woodsy aftershave. *Please don't let me make a fool of myself again.*

"You must be the shy, skittish sister." His chuckle floated to her ears as though she were in a daze.

Cassie laughed. "Just wait till you get to know her. Del's about as shy as a seagull at a picnic."

His dancing gaze held hers as a balmy ocean breeze played with strands of his thick, dark hair. "I look forward to the opportunity . . . to get to know you, I mean." He finally looked at her older sisters and smiled at them. "Have a nice lunch, ladies."

"Ooh, nice." Cassie watched him stride toward the brunette, who waited in a small silver car.

"Wonderful." Brianna added.

Delaney yanked at her sisters' arms and pulled them toward the entrance of the Nautical Nymph Inn. "Let's eat."

After a waitress showed them to a table next to a large window with an expansive view of the sound and took their beverage order, Delaney opened her menu and began to peruse it.

Brianna leaned across the table. "He wants to get to know you better. That's what he said."

"He looks forward to the opportunity, Del."

"He would be just ideal for you."

Delaney ignored the remarks and stared at her menu. *Fresh grilled tuna. Sautéed sea scallops.*

With an exaggerated sigh, Delaney set her menu on the table and gazed around at her three well-meaning, but meddling sisters. "We're here to have lunch, not to discuss the plumber."

"He likes you, Del."

Cassie took a bread stick and passed the basket to Allison. "I think you should go out with him."

"He's probably married."

Allison shook her head. "He's not wearing a wedding band."

"Maybe plumbers don't wear rings. Maybe they get caught on the wrenches or pipes."

Cassie rolled her eyes. "Don't make excuses."

"I'm not. I'm here for a nice, relaxing beach vacation, not for a man-fishing trip."

Chapter Two

"I've been thinking." Allison glanced across the table at the Nautical Nymph Inn and directed her eyes at Delaney. "Gareth Collins may be just the one for you. I have a good feeling about him. In fact, I'd bet a whole month's salary that you'll be engaged before school lets out in December for Christmas break."

Delaney stopped, with her glass of sweet tea halfway to her lips. She stared in shock as the others nodded and shook hands while they increased the bet with wagers that included promises of home-cooked meals, babysitting service, and potential wedding dates. She tried to assure herself that she was the only single sibling present. Allison could not have been addressing anyone but her.

"I wish you would stop all of this talk about marriage.

24

Starting a serious relationship really isn't a priority for me right now. I'm completely content with my life the way it is." Delaney's stomach churned as the waitress arrived to take their orders. Nothing sounded good anymore, except maybe a three-layer chocolate cake and a half gallon of mint-chocolate-chip ice cream.

"I'll have a bowl of Hatteras clam chowder and a soft-shelled crab sandwich. With fries and a pickle." Delaney handed the waitress her menu. "And I'd like to see your dessert list when you get a chance."

"Oh, that sounds good." Brianna rubbed her stomach. "I'll take the same with an order of onion rings."

Allison touched Delaney's arm when the waitress had left their table. "Now, about your wedding plans."

"I have no wedding plans. I'm happy just the way things are."

"You don't look happy, Delaney."

"No, you look tired and overworked," Brianna added.

"I've never seen you with such circles under your eyes," Allison persisted. "What you need, Del, is a nice, quiet vacation here on the Outer Banks with a friendly, attractive, intelligent companion like Gareth Collins."

Delaney reached for another breadstick. "I don't need a man to be happy."

"Maybe not." Allison patted her hand. "But we think it's what you want, even if *you* don't know it's what you want yet."

Delaney shook her head. "What did you just say?"

Cassie leaned toward her from across the table. "I

think what Allison is trying to say is that wanting and needing are two different things. You don't necessarily *need* a man in your life, but sharing it with a man like Gareth could give you a kind of happiness you can't even imagine yet. And we all want you to be happy, Del."

Brianna nibbled a breadstick. "We've decided that Gareth Collins and you are just perfect for each other. He fits right into our plans for you."

"But they're *your* plans, not mine." Delaney was more than a little irritated with her sisters right then, but she realized, with a sinking feeling, that three-against-one were not good odds. She didn't even have a chance. She had already lost if her sisters were as determined as they sounded, but Delaney could be determined too. She had been born with the same Sutton tenacity that they had. Inhaling a deep breath, she tried to explain. "The fact that I'm a professional firefighter scares men away, and I refuse to give up my career just to get married."

"We're not expecting you to give up your job, Del."

"But guys *do* expect it. First, I get a look of amusement, then shock, then annoyance. They suggest it's just a phase I'm going through. All it will take to get the silly idea out of my system is for one of them to put a ring on my finger and rescue me."

"Oh, but the man who truly loves you, your ideal man, will accept you for who you are, Delaney, a committed Richmond firefighter."

The waitress arrived with their meals. As everyone began to eat, Delaney's older sisters appeared to forget, at least for the moment, the subject of Gareth Collins.

Delaney dipped her spoon into the steaming bowl of chowder and heaved a quiet sigh. She hoped someone would bring up another conversation topic.

Swallowing a handful of French fries, Cassie licked her fingers and stirred her lemonade with the straw as she looked across the table at Delaney. "Maybe it's your strategy that's wrong. Maybe you shouldn't tell guys about your work until they get to know you for who you really are."

Uh-oh. Losing all hope that lunch would be relaxing and enjoyable, Delaney set her spoon on the table. "I've tried that too, but then they get angry and act like they've been deceived. I don't like omitting the truth about my work. I'm proud of what I do." She sighed. "I don't think it's fair to me to have to keep an important detail about my life from someone just because it might wound his pride or upset his masculinity."

Brianna chewed a large bite of her crab sandwich and swallowed. "Well, it certainly won't do you any harm to give Gareth a chance, will it?"

"No, it won't." Allison dipped her fork into her lobster salad. "You can't know how he'll react to your career if you never get to know him."

Cassie nodded. "Date. Engagement. Wedding. In that order."

"There isn't going to be a wedding." Delaney pushed the words through her clenched teeth. She was becoming really annoyed.

Allison patted her shoulder. "Don't worry. You have enough to think about right now with your planning and preparing for tonight's party. Cassie, Bri, and I will all help you work things out with Gareth. Don't worry."

Don't worry? My sisters are my own worst enemies. She let a verbal response fade on her lips as she glanced around the table at the nodding blond heads and smiling faces of the other three Suttons. It was no use. They would not listen. They never did.

On the ride back to Avon, Delaney made some mental notes of what she needed for her assigned Sisterhood Sojourn evening: *groceries, colorful silk flowers, paper umbrellas for fruit drinks.*

By five minutes to six, Delaney had set the wicker table on the porch off the kitchen with a floral tablecloth and vases of fresh-cut flowers. Inside the house, she was chilling shrimp salad and a papaya dessert, and she had chicken marinating in the refrigerator.

On the stereo in the family room, she began to play one of her father's old LPs entitled *Sounds of the Hawaiian Islands.* Low electric guitar music and soft drum beats floated through the air.

Delaney ushered her sisters into the room. They were all barefoot and wrapped in colorful curtains she had found in one of the bedroom closets. Leis of silk flowers hung around their necks. The four sat around a low table at one end of the family room as Delaney poured hot green tea with ginger into cups without handles and distributed them before passing around a plate of crisp wafers cut in triangular shapes.

Cassie bit into the treat and chewed. "Mmm. Apricots, bananas, cinnamon."

"These are delicious, Delaney," Allison told her.

"Oh, and the ginger in the tea is a nice touch." Brianna set her cup on the table and reached for a second fruit wedge. "Good job, little sister."

Smiling, Delaney took a sip of tea and brushed crumbs from her fingers. "Now, for some entertainment. You're each going to perform a hula dance for us."

"A hula dance? Are you serious, Del?"

Brianna wrinkled her nose as she flounced the yards of fabric tied around her swollen waist. I don't think I can hula very well."

Cassie nodded. "Bri's got a point. Let's just have a nice quiet evening together."

"Only after you each perform a fairy-tale pantomime to Dad's old Hawaiian music while I take your pictures."

"Our pictures?" Brianna shook her head. "No, please, Delaney. Not in this curtain!"

Delaney grinned. "I may be persuaded to trade tonight's pictures for the tutu video."

Brianna narrowed her eyes and opened her mouth to speak again, but Allison touched her shoulder and stopped her. The eldest Sutton turned to Delaney and smiled. "We'll be good participants." Allison turned to Delaney. "As you've pointed out, you've always been a good sport for us and our silly ideas. I'll go first. Should I choose a fairy tale myself, or are you going to assign one to me?"

"You pick one, and then I'll be able to guess too. Now, remember, you have to use body movements and hand gestures to pantomime the story, just like a hula's done."

"Oh, let me go first. If you're going to make me do this, I want to get it over with." Brianna struggled to her feet. "I can't believe you're forcing a seven-and-a-half-month-pregnant woman to do a hula."

"It'll be fun, Bri," Cassie said. "Del'll take a picture to show my new little nephew."

Brianna narrowed her eyes again. "What makes you think we're having a boy?"

Cassie shrugged. "It seems to me that Will is planning on a boy. He talks about taking his *son* to games and coaching his *son's* team. He's already bought a baseball mitt and an Orioles cap."

Brianna shook her head. "We told the doctor we didn't want to know, but I'm sure this baby's a girl. Allison and Zach have two girls. Mom and Dad had four girls." She rubbed her abdomen. "I'm certain this little one is a girl. Oh, I hope Will won't be disappointed. Are you sure he said *son,* not *child?*" Brianna's face had a stricken expression as she grasped Allison's arm. "Oh, what if he doesn't really like our daughter? What if

Will doesn't get close to her because, deep down, he always wanted our first child to be a son?"

"Now, Bri, calm down." Allison slipped her arm around Brianna's slumped shoulders. "You're getting yourself upset over something that hasn't even happened yet. You know that Will and you will love this baby whether your child is a boy or a girl." She hugged Brianna. "Now, we're supposed to be having a good time tonight. This is the first evening of the Sutton Sisterhood Sojourn weekend, and Delaney has spent a lot of time and energy preparing for it. Maybe you'd like someone else to dance first."

A twist of guilt tightened in Delaney's stomach. Poor Brianna. She probably should have been more understanding of her pregnant sister's feelings when she'd insisted that Brianna dance.

"Here, let me show you." Delaney hugged Brianna too, and then helped her sit down on a big pillow on the floor. "I'll give you an idea of what I had in mind. And I promise not to take any pictures."

A melody of stringed instruments filled the family room as Delaney increased the volume and took a place in front of the low table around which her sisters had taken seats again. With teary eyes, Brianna munched another fruit wedge and smiled at her. Cassie and Allison clapped and cheered with loud, encouraging words.

"Dance for us, Del."

"Show us how to do the hula."

Inhaling a slow, calming breath, Delaney straightened

her lei of silk flowers and, in her bare feet, began to sway to the music from the stereo. The bottom of her flower curtain swung with her. She moved her arms as though she were sweeping and then pretended to primp in front of an imaginary mirror.

"*Sleeping Beauty!*" Cassie shouted out her guess.

Delaney shook her head and glanced at her wrist. Then she covered her mouth with her hands and hurried back and forth in front of the table several times.

"*Snow White!*"

"*Beauty and the Beast!*"

Frowning, she shook her head again. She thought they were just naming fairy tales without really concentrating on her pantomimes. She pretended to sit on the edge of a chair; and, crossing one leg over the other, she stuck out her bare foot and pretended to slip on a make-believe shoe.

"*Cinderella*, right?"

Delaney snapped her head around and stared at the entrance to the family room. Her bottom jaw dropped in surprise as she saw the now-familiar face of Gareth Collins smiling back at her.

"It looks like you're acting out *Cinderella* as the prince slides the glass slipper onto her foot."

His quiet voice and expressive blue eyes sent her heartbeat racing. Still in a squatting position, she tried to rise on wobbling legs, but lost her balance. Waving her arms in every direction, she toppled onto the polished hardwood floor.

Feeling her cheeks burn with embarrassment, she sat sprawled with the colorful curtain draped around her like a blanket. She groaned as the room filled with laughter from her older sisters, and Gareth, in his gray uniform and work boots, took a few steps toward her.

"Are you all right?" He gazed down at her with eyes full of concern, although Delaney did not miss the tug of a grin at the corners of his mouth.

She grasped the hand he held out to her and thanked him as he helped her to her feet. "Right." She cleared her throat. "It's *Cinderella*."

She watched him as his eyes studied her from her head to her bare toes and a smile broke across his handsome face. If she had not been so humiliated, she probably would have enjoyed the way he continued to hold her hand long after she was standing on steady feet again.

With his other hand, he reached out to finger a silk lavender orchid on her lei, and his smile broadened. "Nice outfit."

Her sisters began to clap and greet the plumber. They congratulated him for guessing the correct fairy tale and invited him to join them for another pantomime.

Although she thought they were exaggerating with such gushing praise, she forced a smile as he released her hand. "Good guess, Mr. Collins."

His eyebrows lifted a fraction, but he didn't comment on her formality. Instead, he turned to the Sutton sisters still on the floor. "I rang the doorbell, but no one answered. I guess you didn't hear it with the music on."

Allison smiled. "We're having a luau. Would you like some ginger tea?"

He glanced at Delaney and then shook his head. "Thank you, but I just stopped by with the part to repair your washer."

Cassie jumped to her feet. "I'll take you to the laundry room."

Again, he shook his head. "I don't want to interrupt. I remember the way, and I shouldn't be long."

Delaney watched him turn and leave the family room. A vague sense of disappointment washed over her. "I have to put the chicken on to broil."

Cassie rounded the table. "I'll get ready to dance next." She touched Delaney's shoulder. "You okay? You look a little pale. You didn't get hurt when you fell, did you?"

With shaky hands, Delaney secured her curtain wrap. "No, I'm fine. I'll be right back."

After she turned on the broiler and set plates and silverware on the wicker table on the balcony, Delaney returned to the family room where Cassie and Allison each pantomimed a fairy tale. The enthusiasm Delaney had initially experienced for the activity had waned, however, with Brianna's emotional episode and Gareth Collins' unexpected interruption.

"Let's eat." Delaney set the tea pot, cups, and plates on the tray and lifted it from the table. "Dinner's ready."

Cassie turned off the stereo, and Allison helped Brianna to stand up from her seat on the floor. The three older sisters headed for the deck while Delaney remained in the kitchen to fill another tray with serving dishes containing the Hawaiian feast.

Grateful that her heart finally seemed to be beating at a normal rate again, she sat down with her sisters to enjoy the meal she'd prepared. She enjoyed the light, warm ocean breeze blowing across the deck.

As she began to pass dishes around the table, she breathed in the humid sea air and tried to relax. After all, relaxation was her purpose for being on Hatteras Island. Chief Adler had forced her to take vacation to rest and to make a decision about her future. So far, she had not had a chance to think about anything but the handsome plumber repairing their washer.

Cassie speared a shrimp along with slices of orange and cucumber and grinned. "This smells absolutely scrumptious. Where'd you get the recipes for tonight? Your culinary skills typically extend to a file of take-out menus and a chart listing how many minutes needed to heat food in the microwave."

Delaney wrinkled her nose at her. "I found one of Mom's old cookbooks."

"This pineapple chicken is excellent." Allison studied the food on her plate. "Is this cilantro? And there's another taste. Cumin, I think."

Brianna swallowed her last bite of chicken. "I don't know what's in it, but it's delicious. May I have another piece?"

"Slow down, Bri," Cassie said. "Don't you want to

save room for dessert?" She turned to Delaney. "Will you tell us what we're having, or is it a secret?"

Delaney took a drink of ice water. "It's called Tropical Delight—papaya, kiwifruit, lime, and orange juice, all topped with whipped cream."

Brianna sighed. "Sounds heavenly."

"The table looks so pretty, Delaney." Allison smiled at her. "Where did you find all these beautiful fresh flowers?"

"An elderly lady who lives in Buxton has the most marvelous perennial flower garden. I offered to pay her for them, but she refused to take anything. She just wanted me to promise to stop by sometime to visit with her." She slapped her forehead with her hand. "Oh, I forgot the candles. I was going to light candles while we ate as long as it wasn't too windy."

"I'm sure there's some in the laundry room closet." Cassie grinned as she rose from her chair. "I'll get them. It'll give me an excuse to check on Gareth."

Allison shook her head. "I think I heard him leave."

Brianna nodded. "Me too. He probably didn't want to bother us. He's so polite and considerate."

Delaney wiped her mouth with a napkin and stood. A mixture of relief and regret flooded her senses. "I'll find the candles and then get dessert ready. Anybody up for a strawberry-banana smoothie? I have the blender all ready to go."

She entered the beach house through one of the sliding glass doors and hurried up to the third-floor hallway. As she approached the laundry room, she noticed that the louvered doors were still open. She wondered if Gareth had forgotten to close them.

Her bare feet on the hardwood floor made little sound as she reached the end of the hallway. In astonishment, she halted just a few feet from the dryer as two sets of eyes looked at her. One pair, blue-green and narrowed, was accompanied by a loud meow. The other pair, intensely blue, held a sparkling gleam that sent her heart pounding in an unnatural rhythm.

"Aloha, Cinderella."

"Oh!" The exclamation burst from her mouth before Delaney could stop it.

"I was just finishing up." Gareth set some pliers and a screwdriver in his plastic tool box.

She inhaled a deep breath. "You're still here."

"Yes, the repairs took a little longer than I expected, but the washer's running fine now. Your kitty has been keeping me company."

"Kitty?" A thirty-six-inch-long cat? Delaney glanced at Max, who was ignoring her. He sent an adoring gaze at Gareth. *What a traitor!* She reached out and smoothed the fur along his spine. "This is Max. I hope he hasn't been bothering you."

"Not at all." He shut his tool box. "It may be my imagination, but I think we were having a conversation at one point."

Delaney nodded. "He talks when he's happy."

What was going on with Max, her best friend, her

confidant, her roommate? First, he sat with Cassie in the morning, and then he decided to visit with the plumber he had clearly disliked earlier that day. Shaking her head, she turned back in the direction she had come. Nothing was making sense anymore.

"Wait, Delaney. Please." The sound of his quiet voice was almost a caress to her ears.

On unsteady legs, she pivoted on her bare toes to face him again. Inhaling another deep breath to calm her racing heart, she met his smiling face.

"I'm confused." His blue eyes held her gaze. "First, you ran away from me when you saw me this morning. Then you tried to hide behind your sister at the restaurant at lunch. Tonight, you fell and nearly tore your flowery dress when I arrived to repair the washer. Now you're ready to run away again. Have I done something to upset you?"

Upset? She was not sure she would have used that word to describe how she felt, but he definitely affected her. Why? Why did Gareth Collins seem to provoke a combination of feelings so powerful that she couldn't think when he was near?

"Let's start again." His smile warmed her all the way to the tips of her bare toes, and his blue eyes sparkled. "I'm Gareth Collins. I'm helping my sister-in-law with my brother's plumbing-and-air-conditioning business here on Hatteras because he had to have emergency gall bladder surgery two weeks ago and is recuperating now."

Sister-in-law? The brunette at the restaurant?

Allison was right. He was not married. She moistened her suddenly dry lips with the tip of her tongue. "I'm Delaney. Delaney Quincey Sutton. I'm here on vacation with my family." She caught her bottom lip between her teeth for a moment as his scrutinizing eyes appeared to give her their full attention. They seemed able to reach right into her soul. "I'm here with my sisters for our annual weekend get-together."

He lifted dark brows above intense blue eyes. "A sort of family bonding time?"

She nodded as Max stood on his perch on top of the dryer and stretched. She reached out a hand to smooth his multi-colored fur. "To relax, rejuvenate, and reconnect. That's our motto."

"You have a motto?"

Delaney sighed. "You don't know my sisters. They're very serious about this sibling stuff. The rest of our family—Mom and Dad, their husbands, Allison's daughters—they're all coming Tuesday to spend the month, but this weekend is for Sutton sisters only. They call it the Sutton Sisterhood Sojourn."

"And tonight you're celebrating by having a luau?"

She pulled her gaze from his eyes. "Right now we're eating out on the balcony off the kitchen. I came for candles for the table. Would you like something to eat, or maybe a drink? We have fresh pineapple and mango juice, and I have the blender ready to whip up smoothies."

He shook his head as he reached for his tool box. "I still have another stop to make just down the beach from here—a faulty air conditioning unit."

"Plumbers work late."

He nodded. "It took me longer to repair your washer than I thought it would, and I took time to go out for lunch earlier today, so I have to make up the time this evening." He smiled at her once again. "It was very nice to meet you, Delaney. Maybe I'll see you again."

For the remainder of the evening, Delaney visited with her sisters as they ate the papaya dessert she had prepared, sipped on fruit smoothies, cleared the table, and washed the dishes. Then she lounged on a deck chair and listened to stories of her sisters' families, their jobs, and their lives. They caught up on everything that had happened to them since they'd been together for Cassie's wedding a month before.

She closed her eyes as Brianna talked about one of the lawyers in the firm where she worked as a paralegal in Durham. Cassie discussed an important highway project on which she was working as a civil engineer in Raleigh.

Delaney had not wanted to take a vacation, but that evening as she listened to the sound of the surf and smelled the salty sea air, she decided that she was glad she had come to stay on the Outer Banks of North Carolina. Of course, she still did not agree with Chief Adler that she needed to reconsider the direction of her future as a firefighter, but the prospect of spending a long weekend with her exuberant sisters made her feel more relaxed than she had in months.

At midnight, when she went to the room she shared with Cassie, at least until Cassie's husband arrived, she tumbled into bed and hoped her sister was tired too. She must have fallen asleep as soon as her head touched her pillow because the last thing she remembered after saying good night to Cassie was cuddling up to Max and closing her eyes.

Delaney sat straight up in bed and stared into the darkness. Something had awakened her, another dream probably, but she could not recall why it had been so frightening. Max moved and readjusted his position on her feet as she lay her head on her pillow and closed her eyes.

She must have fallen asleep again because the next time she opened her eyes, she could feel the cat stretched out beside her, but the darkness still filled the room. It was starting again.

She'd thought that the trip to Hatteras Island would help her mind break the pattern of waking up repeatedly and never getting more than an hour of sleep at a time. The previous night she had slept. She believed the ocean air and supportive company of her sisters had finally soothed her subconscious so she could get a normal night's sleep.

For months in Richmond, she had awakened several

times each night and then tossed and turned for some time before finally drifting off to sleep again. When she *had* slept, it was never restful. The dream she had over and over again, about the unidentified firefighter she tried to rescue, tortured her thoughts until she awoke the next time.

A lack of restful sleep was the reason she had panicked in the warehouse that morning Chief Adler had called her into his office. She had not had a good night's rest for almost eight months. At first, she'd been able to hide the fact that she couldn't give her best effort to her work; but the lack of sleep was now beginning to affect her performance.

The chief was right about that. She simply wasn't doing the best job that she could. She had to face that fact, but not being able to sleep well at night still didn't mean that she wanted to change her profession.

"Wake up, sleepyhead! I'm not going to let you stay in bed till eleven again today."

Delaney opened her eyes to the sound of Cassie's voice as her sister bounced on the foot of the twin bed. She took a moment to clear her mind.

She'd been dreaming: There had been an explosion in a warehouse. Most of the fire was out, but she stumbled in the dim light and almost tripped over a fallen firefighter. She leaned down to remove his mask, and a familiar face flashed a smile at her. Gareth Collins. Not only had he smiled, but he'd spoke to her too. *"Hi, De-laney. Nice outfit."*

She looked down, and instead of her bunker pants and boots, she wore a curtain of floral fabric and her feet were bare.

"Come on. Go take your shower so we can start the day. I'm in the mood for blueberry pancakes and sausage for breakfast. I think I smell bacon cooking already too." Cassie stopped bouncing and scooped Max into her arms. Changing the topic, but still chattering, she remarked, "The drain in our bathroom is a little sluggish. Tim and I'll be moving into the bedroom across the hall when he gets here on Tuesday, so we'll use the bathroom there, but you'll still have this slow drain to contend with. We might have to call Gareth again."

Oh, no. Delaney pulled the pillow over her head. Not another potentially embarrassing encounter with the island plumber. She didn't think she could take much more humiliation.

Chapter Three

In the approaching dusk of Saturday, Delaney looked around the wicker table at her sisters, who each wore long strings of plastic purple, amber, and green beads around their necks. Talking, laughing, and enjoying the Mardi Gras evening that Allison had planned, they didn't seem to notice her lack of enthusiasm.

She'd barely touched her black beans and brown rice and had eaten only a small portion of her Creole sandwich, a delicious mixture of flaky catfish, tomato sauce, chopped peppers, and onions on slices of warm corn bread. She sipped iced tea and forced a smile as Cassie, sitting across the table from her, finished a long, hilarious story about a poodle that followed her home from the park one day.

Cassie narrowed her eyes and studied Delaney. "Where *are* you tonight?"

On Delaney's left side, Brianna put a spoonful of black beans and rice on her plate. "You seem a little distracted."

On Delaney's other side, Allison patted her arm. "What's wrong?"

"I'm fine." She set her glass on the table. "Just a little tired, I guess."

Cassie's beads brushed the table's surface as she leaned toward her and set her elbows on the tablecloth. "You look as though you haven't had a good night's sleep in months. What's going on?"

"Nothing's going on." She did not want to tell her sisters that she hadn't slept a whole night without waking up since the fire and explosion that had killed her fellow firefighter, Hal Barker, the previous year.

She was not ready to tell them about Chief Adler's order that she take time off from work to make an important decision about her future. She definitely did not want to tell them that, in addition to the problems she'd brought to Hatteras Island, Gareth Collins had been the subject of both her dreams at night and her thoughts during the day.

"Oh, come on, Del. You can tell us."

Allison squeezed her arm. "I'm sure we can help if you tell us what's bothering you."

Brianna nodded as she finished chewing a forkful of rice. "We have lots of good ideas."

Cassie clapped her hands. "I think I know what's wrong. You need a date."

Delaney groaned. *Not that subject again.*

Allison smiled. "Let's leave Delaney alone. As soon as I clean up the kitchen, we're heading to the Driftwood Grill for the second part of our evening."

"The Driftwood Grill?" Brianna lifted her gold-colored half-mask to her eyes. "Are we wearing our beads and masks?"

"Probably not the masks, but I think the beads will be a nice touch to our attire. I decided we'd skip dessert here so we'll have room for the Driftwood's crab cakes and Cajun fried shrimp appetizers. I know you can't drink, Bri but we can have seltzer water or fruit juice and listen to the band that plays there on Saturday night."

Delaney shook her head. "I think I'll just stay in and do a little reading tonight."

"Oh, you have to come, Del. This is part of the celebration. You can't back out."

"It'll be fun." Brianna finally decided to eat the last sandwich. "You've always loved the crab cakes at the Driftwood."

Allison patted her arm. "We won't stay late—I promise. We'll just go and relax and listen to the country music."

Against Delaney's better judgment, she agreed to accompany her three older sisters. She was not in the mood to go out in public, especially with a bunch of plastic beads dangling from her neck; but the crab cakes there were renowned. Since she hadn't had dessert, she could probably afford the extra calories.

The night was clear and the sky full of stars as Allison drove into the gravel parking area in front of the popular waterfront restaurant. It was a one-story structure that stood at ground level with three floors of open porches and stairways leading to a large lookout platform at the top. Around the outside edge of the fourth level were built-in benches for patrons who were willing to climb the steps for a breath of sea air and a view of both the sound and the ocean. Already, several cars had lined the spaces near the entrance and had begun to fill up around the perimeter of the large lot.

"Look at all the people here." Delaney stepped from the back seat of her oldest sister's vehicle. "You promised it would be quiet tonight."

Brianna shrugged. "I guess she was mistaken. Come on. I can smell that Cajun shrimp frying."

Cassie tossed Delaney her lightweight cardigan. "Don't forget this. I don't want you complaining about the air conditioning and wanting to leave before we get our first basket of crab cakes."

Brianna slipped an arm around Delaney's waist and urged her in the direction of the front door. "She's not going to have a chance to get cold because she'll be dancing to every song with one of the many handsome, eligible men here tonight."

Delaney stopped and stared at Brianna, and then sent

warning looks to Allison and Cassie. "Oh, no. If that's the plan, to hook me up with a stranger, then I'm not even going in."

"You'll just have to sit out here and wait for us." Allison jangled her car keys in the air before slipping them into the pocket of her shorts. "The Sutton sisters came together, and we'll leave together. That's the rule."

"Then I'll walk home."

With wide gray eyes, Cassie gazed at her. "You'd rather walk back to the beach house than take a chance that you might meet someone nice this evening?"

Delaney glanced down at the sandals she'd worn with her printed Capri pants and sleeveless knit top. She wasn't exactly prepared to travel on foot. Sighing, she spoke with much less conviction than she would have liked. "If I had to, I would. I'm not dancing, so get that idea out of your heads right now."

Allison linked one of her arms through one of Delaney's. "We promise we won't push you to get on the dance floor with anyone you don't want to be with. We'll just . . . survey the prospects."

Delaney shook her head. "Oh, no. That sounds even more ominous than the dreaded blind dates you've sent me on."

Cassie led the group toward the door. If Allison and Brianna hadn't had their arms linked with Delaney's and been pulling her forward, she might have lost her nerve and headed back to the beach house on foot— despite her inappropriate footwear.

The sisters led her to a corner table on a raised floor of the one-story building. From her seat, she could see the bar at one end and the late evening diners who sat at tables around its outside edge. In the center of the room, a few couples swayed to a slow, familiar country melody of fiddle and guitar music that was being played by a band on the far side of the large, open space.

"Isn't that Gareth?" Cassie almost stood from her chair as she strained to see the tall, dark man sitting alone several tables down from them. "He's eating alone."

"That's too bad." Brianna tossed a handful of buttered popcorn in her mouth and chewed.

Allison shook her head. "What a waste."

Cassie sighed. "You're telling me. That man can work wonders with pliers and a wrench."

"Plumbers get paid very well." Allison fingered a piece of fluffy popcorn as she sent him an admiring glance. "Just think of all the money the Suttons could save if we had a plumber in the family."

Delaney rolled her eyes. "We don't have a doctor in the family. We could use one of those."

Cassie licked butter from her fingers. "Maybe, but a doctor is not eating alone three tables from us. A plumber is."

"Let's order some baskets of crab cakes and forget about plumbers."

Brianna sighed. "He looks so lonely sitting there by himself."

Cassie nodded. "We should invite him to join us."

"That's a wonderful idea," Allison agreed.

"No, it's not. Don't you dare."

Brianna took another handful of popcorn from the plastic bowl. "We can't just let him eat by himself."

Delaney shook her head. "Maybe he likes being alone."

"Who likes eating alone?" Cassie said.

Allison glanced in Gareth's direction. "Maybe one of us *should* go over and invite him to sit with us."

"I vote for Del to do it."

"Me too," Brianna agreed with Cassie.

"No, I won't. You can't make me." Delaney realized she sounded like a child again arguing with her older sisters about doing some outrageous activity in which they had decided she should participate. With a deep sigh, she shook her head again. "Let's just leave him to eat in peace. I'm sure he's had a long day."

Three pairs of gray eyes turned to look at her.

"He has had a very long day, Del."

"He'd probably appreciate an invitation to join in some casual conversation that doesn't relate to clogged sinks and broken air conditioners."

Brianna poked her elbow into Delaney's ribs. "Oh, stop being such a chicken. Go and ask him to come and sit with us."

"No!" Her emphatic refusal seemed to resound against the walls of the wooden structure as the band finished a fast country song. Delaney snapped her head in Gareth's direction to make sure he hadn't heard, and her heart did a little somersault in her chest.

He *had* noticed. In fact, he was looking back at her and smiling.

Even across the distance, his blue eyes read her thoughts; or, at least, they appeared to be clairvoyant for a moment. He lifted his arm and waved.

She whipped her head around so fast that her neck hurt, and she saw all three of her sisters return his wave. *Oh, great! What does he think of the Sutton family now?*

Brianna nudged her again. "Go on. Make your move, little sister."

Delaney shook her head. "I have no moves. I will make no moves. It's a mistake to be here. I never should have agreed to come with you tonight."

"It wasn't a mistake, Del."

"It was destiny," Allison said. "What better way is there to get you two together than on the dance floor? Can't you see that fate is working in your favor this evening?"

Cassie nodded. "It's the beads."

Delaney inhaled a long, steady breath. "It's the three meddling sisters. That's all it is—not destiny, not fate, and certainly not how I want to conduct my social life."

"We're not talking about your social life anymore, Del. Now it's the serious stuff. Allison made a bet. You have to be engaged by the end of the school term. That's the wager."

Delaney closed her eyes and tried to ignore the uneasiness pressing against her from all sides. Her sisters were stubborn. All of them, including Delaney, had been born with the Sutton determination that their ideas and perspectives were the best choices to make, given certain circumstances.

Because they had Delaney's paramount interest at heart, the older ones always believed that if they persisted in their attempts to persuade her, eventually she would come to the conclusion that they were right; but she had to stop them now. The preposterous prediction that she would be engaged by Christmas to a man to whom she had barely spoken two sentences was getting out of hand.

"How's the washer?"

Delaney swallowed. Had she just imagined Gareth Collins' low baritone voice speaking just above the soft notes of a slow country ballad? Cautiously, she opened her eyes. Air swished from her lungs and left her feeling as though the room no longer had any oxygen at all. He was standing right next to Cassie's chair. His dark blue eyes, with their penetrating gaze, focused on Delaney.

"Better than ever," Allison replied. "We did two loads of beach towels and blankets before we came."

"So the Sutton sisters are out on the town tonight?"

Cassie lifted her green, purple, and amber beads and twirled them in front of her. "We're here to party New Orleans style. Have you ever been to a Mardi Gras celebration, Gareth?"

A broad grin spread across his handsome face, and Delaney's heart did a little flutter. *Wow!* Had she noticed what a nice mouth he had, how perfect it was for kissing? *Kissing?* What was she thinking? She was in a restaurant, gawking at the man who had repaired her family's washing machine. *Get a grip, Delaney!*

His chuckle rumbled from him as he shook his head and flashed a set of perfect, white teeth. "I can't say that I have—at least, not in July."

"Well, sit down and join us." Brianna swept her hand toward an empty chair. "It's Allison's night to plan the theme, and she arranged a Mardi Gras party. We're just getting ready to order crab cakes and spicy fried shrimp."

He patted the front of his white polo shirt above the place where his brown leather belt circled the low waistband of his khaki shorts. "I just had a whole basket of fried clams and a double order of cole slaw."

Allison smiled. "Then have a drink with us. Our treat."

He lifted dark brows above sparkling blue eyes. "Trying to bribe the plumber. I think there's a rule against that."

"Ooh, a man who follows rules." Brianna slid an empty chair toward him. "That's great! Here, sit down right next to Delaney. She could use some lessons in following rules."

What is that supposed to mean? Still puzzled by her sister's remark, she glanced up at him.

For a moment, his eyes locked with hers. Air rushed from her lungs and left her breathless and dizzy.

Wishing she could disappear, she felt her heart skip a

beat at his nearness. Heat radiated from him when his tanned forearm brushed hers as he sat down at the small circular table.

Trying to breathe in a room that had become a vacuum, she wondered what was going through his mind. Did he think all of the Suttons were crazy? After all, they'd actually admitted that they were celebrating Mardi Gras on Hatteras Island in July. They were wearing strands of beads—plastic purple, green, and amber beads.

A waitress arrived and took their order for baskets of crab cakes, and Cajun fried shrimp, and ice-cold sodas. Gareth ordered a glass of seltzer water.

"What exactly does that mean?" He smiled at Delaney as the waitress left. "Are you really a nonconformist?"

"No."

"Don't believe her. Del takes rebellion to a whole new level."

"She a maverick," Allison added.

"Whatever we do, she does the opposite," Brianna said. "We like dogs, so Delaney gets a cat."

"We always want white cake for our birthdays, but Del has to have chocolate."

Allison sighed. "We all belonged to the swim team in high school, but our baby sister had to play soccer."

"And when it was time for college, we went to Dad's alma mater, Duke University, but Delaney decided to go to—"

"—Virginia Commonwealth University."

Delaney joined her sisters in staring at him in surprise. Her heart jumped when he flashed a grin.

"A lucky guess." He shrugged broad shoulders beneath the cotton knit fabric of his shirt. "I noticed your tee shirt yesterday morning before you ducked back into your bedroom." He turned from her to smile at the others seated around the table. "So, what you're really telling me is that Delaney doesn't follow the rules that the *Sutton sisters* have established."

Brianna nodded. "The Suttons should always stick together."

"Our baby sister fights tradition simply to be different," Allison said.

He lifted dark brows above sparkling blue eyes that gazed at Delaney. "Maybe she is."

Cassie shook her head. "Del's just a rebel, but we love her and want her to be happy."

Brianna held up her glass of ginger ale. "Let's make a toast."

Delaney lifted her glass automatically, but did not feel as though she belonged to the group at the moment. Her head was spinning, and her hand shook.

Gareth raised his glass with the others. "What are we drinking to?"

"To Delaney's happiness."

"To Delaney's happiness."

Cassie and Brianna giggled as their simultaneous toast rang through the air above the music of the band. They touched their glasses together.

Delaney groaned under her breath. She wanted to slide beneath the table and disappear; but she knew, with her luck, that the trap door she found would probably lead right to the center of the dance floor, where she'd face even more humiliation.

To her relief, their waitress delivered the crab cakes and shrimp, and she hoped the conversation would turn away from her. She bit into the hot, crisp outer layer and enjoyed the fluffy inner layer of the crab cake while her sisters helped themselves to the delicious snacks from the large cloth-lined baskets in the center of the table.

"Do you like to dance, Gareth?"

Delaney nearly choked as Brianna's innocent tone sparked every nerve in her body. She tried not to look directly at the man to her right as she caught a glimpse of his expression. Did he realize that he was like a sand castle—just sitting there waiting to be swept away by the powerful, conniving waves of the Sutton sisters? He probably had no idea what was coming his way.

His smile sent her stomach into a series of somer-saulting flutters.

"Actually, I prefer to listen, especially to fast numbers like this one. I've never taken time to learn all of those complicated steps."

There. That should do it. Gareth doesn't dance.

Brianna formed her mouth into a sweet smile that Delaney knew meant trouble. She passed a basket of spicy fried shrimp to her and hoped the aroma would entice Brianna to eat more and talk less.

"But you'd dance if someone you were with wanted to, right?"

Delaney cringed and tried to catch Brianna's eyes. *Please. Don't. Stop before it's too late.*

His smile broadened to reveal those perfect white teeth in that perfect mouth that appeared just perfect for kissing. *Kissing? Again?*

"Well, I always try to be polite to the people I'm with. Would you like to dance, Brianna?"

"Me? Oh, no, not me, but Delaney here—" Brianna nudged her with her elbow.

Delaney shook her head. "No, I wouldn't." Her heart sank as her voice cracked, and she realized that her response lacked conviction.

Gareth reached out and touched her hand. Tiny sparks energized her nerves.

She lifted her eyes to meet his gaze. *Snap!* She felt as though he held her with some kind of invisible force. Somewhere in the background, beyond the racing of her heart and the somersaulting of her stomach, she heard the band finish the fast country melody and begin to play a slow, romantic one. Gareth's intense blue eyes still held hers as his hand caressed her fingers.

"Dance with me, Delaney?" His request possessed a certain enchantment she found difficult to resist. His quiet, baritone voice had a mesmerizing quality that fascinated her despite her resolve to stay right where she was.

On impulse, she rose from her chair and allowed him to lead her down the steps onto the floor in front of the band. She felt like Cinderella agreeing to dance with Prince Charming at the ball; but instead of having evil stepsisters foiling her attempts to meet her true love, Delaney had three overly attentive and interfering sisters pushing her toward mounting embarrassment because they were sure they knew what was best for her.

She barely heard the song the band was playing as Gareth's arm encircled her. His hand settled on a sensitive spot in the middle of her back as he urged her to experience the rhythm of the music with him. With fluid movements, he seemed to lead her without effort around the dance floor. His gentle hold on her gave her a sense of complete comfort and security in a situation that should have evoked distress and agitation.

In her flat leather sandals, she didn't even reach his shoulders. Had she noticed before how tall he was?

She felt the strength of his smooth, muscular arms as she glided with him in a room that no longer seemed full of people, and sounds, and activity. Gareth Collins and she were all alone in a formless place, as though they were floating together, just the two of them, in one of her dreams.

She tried to relax her breathing. Where had all the air gone? Her head spun as she inhaled the subtle scent of his soap and aftershave.

With a deep, calming breath, she tilted her head until she saw his blue eyes looking down at her. For a moment, his gaze held hers again with that mysterious control he seemed to have.

She moistened her dry lips with the tip of her tongue. "Uh, you're not doing badly for someone who doesn't like to dance."

When he smiled, his face seemed to light up with such warmth that Delaney felt wrapped in a state of contentment and tranquility that she had not experienced for a very long time. If he could make her feel so good with a single smile, then she wondered about the possible effects he could elicit when his mouth actually touched hers as they kissed. *What? Kisses again?* She swallowed. What was going on? Why was her mind roaming to such absurd places? Realizing that she was still staring at him, she blinked.

His smile widened, and his deep blue eyes sparkled. "You're doing quite well too."

"Me?"

"I sensed some hesitation on your part when Brianna suggested the idea."

"I came for the crab cakes."

"The Driftwood has the best on Hatteras Island."

She nodded. "I wasn't going to come, but I like the crab cakes here. I only came to eat the crab cakes."

"So you said."

She knew she was rambling, but she couldn't seem to make her mouth say what she really wanted to say.

What *did* she want to say to this handsome stranger who was holding her in his arms? She licked her lips again. "They tricked me."

"Your sisters?"

"Yes. I'm fairly sure the crab cakes weren't the only reason they had in persuading me to come here tonight."

His blue eyes glittered with obvious understanding. "It appears that your sisters may have had other motives."

Delaney nodded. "Without a doubt."

"They wanted to be sure you're having a good time, perhaps?"

"Oh, it's much more complicated than that. As usual, the Sutton sisters have a whole, elaborate scheme going."

"A scheme involving their youngest sister?"

She nodded. "One they deem will set me on the road to true love and happiness."

He adjusted his hand in the middle of her back and sent tiny pulses up and down her spine. He leaned toward her and spoke near her ear as his breath brushed across her cheek. "Tell me."

She rolled her eyes. "You would never believe it."

Gareth continued to lead her in small, smooth circles around the dance floor as the band transitioned to a slow ballad. He moved with a natural tempo that relaxed her tense muscles and uneasiness.

Her legs felt shaky, and she had a hard time concentrating on the placement of her feet. *Please don't let me stumble or step on his toes.*

Keeping his arms around her in a hold so close that she could feel the cadence of his breathing, he pulled his head far enough away to look down into her eyes again. "You and your sisters seem to have a wonderful, close relationship."

Delaney smiled. "Yes, I suppose we do."

"I don't know much about sisters. In my family, there are just my brother and me. We never had weekend get-togethers, even before Nate got married."

"Are the two of you close?"

"I guess we are. We still take time every year to go to Baltimore for an Orioles game or two."

"You're an Orioles fan?" *Just wait until the sisters hear that. It's one more positive point for Gareth Collins.*

He nodded. "We also try to fit in a day of fishing during the summer. Now, though, most of Nate's time off work is filled with activities involving Jessica and his daughters—soccer matches, dance recitals, science fairs, church events."

Delaney sighed. "That's what happens as we get older and our families grow larger."

He moved his hand across her back and sent a surge of delightful sensations through her. She inhaled a long, unsteady breath as she tried to calm her racing heart. One more dance would probably turn her into a limp pile on the floor in front of the band.

"But—"

Realizing he was waiting for her to respond, she swallowed. *What were we talking about?* "Um, we've been lucky, I guess. We Sutton sisters are still close, even after we've all moved out of our parents' house and started separate lives."

"Being close is good, right?"

She tried to concentrate on her feet. Her knees felt so weak. "Usually, but sometimes, like tonight, it's kind of a nuisance." She sighed again. "I mean, marriages and in-laws and children don't seem to impede my sisters' attempts to secure what they perceive as my ultimate happiness."

He smiled. "Are you saying that, even though they have your best interests in mind, they can be a bit overbearing at times?"

She almost stopped dancing as she gazed up into his expressive eyes. "Exactly." She cleared her throat. "Not many people *get* that. Others tend to believe that having a close family has no disadvantages." *Do you really understand? Have I finally met someone who listens to me and understands me too?* Delaney sighed. She should not get her hopes up too high.

She hadn't told him the big news yet. More than likely, Gareth Collins was just like every other man she had ever liked. They understood her to a point, but then became completely intolerant at soon as she told them about her profession.

The music slowed and ended. Gareth dropped one arm, but kept his other around her waist. "So, about this Sutton sister scheme. Was my dancing with you a part of that?"

Delaney met his gaze. The room felt so warm. Should she tell him about Allison's prediction and the bet the others had made about her being engaged by Christmas? After all, Gareth was as much a victim as she was in this whole Sutton sister romantic plot.

"You look flushed, Delaney. Are you all right?" He looked down at her with concern in his deep blue eyes. "Would you like to go outdoors for some fresh air?"

Chapter Four

The refreshing sea air cooled Delaney's face and arms as she stepped out the side door of the Driftwood Grill. Her awareness of Gareth Collins' nearness made her nerves tingle in anticipation of feelings she did not want to acknowledge. She shivered as the balmy air touched her damp skin. Tipping her head, she looked up at the night sky. "The moon's so bright tonight."

His arm brushed hers as he stopped beside her. "A perfect island evening."

Turning, she gazed at him. "Let's go up to the top deck. I haven't climbed there since last year."

"I saw a rope across the steps. The management must have painted them recently."

She headed toward the open stairs leading to the roof of the restaurant. "Then we can use the ladder."

"The ladder?" He followed her. "That's just for emergencies."

Delaney wrinkled her nose as she stared at the WET PAINT sign dangling from a rope strung across the railing near the bottom step. "This *is* an emergency. I need to see the moon from the top deck."

"There's nothing to hold on to for three stories except those flat wooden rungs. The ladder goes straight up, Delaney. It's not safe—"

She grasped the four-inch, rough-hewn slat at eye level and mounted the bottom rung of the ladder secured to the side of the Driftwood Grill. Grabbing on to the board above her head, she began to climb.

She moved with confidence and determination on steady legs. The night breeze blew stronger as she ascended. She heard Gareth following her, but it didn't matter. She didn't care if she had company or not. She wanted to reach the top deck and feel the exhilaration of the physical exercise of scaling a building and the potential danger of being three stories above the ground without a safety net or harness to protect her.

She climbed at a quick, continuous pace without stopping to rest. When she stepped onto the top deck, outlined with benches built along the perimeter, her lungs begged for oxygen and her heart raced from the exertion.

Leaning against the railing, she breathed in the humid sea air and tipped her head back to feel the breeze blow across her warm face and through loose strands of hair. Even with the bright light of the moon, she couldn't see the ocean, but she heard the waves as they rushed against the beach just across the highway, beyond a row of multi-level beach houses.

"I'm impressed."

She turned at the sound of Gareth's quiet voice. She had almost forgotten he was still with her.

"I can see you're not afraid of heights. Do you swing from a trapeze and walk a tightrope, too?"

Delaney laughed because she felt free and alive. She almost told him then, almost revealed the one aspect about her life that was bound to complicate any relationship she had with a man. She wanted to be honest with him and to share the part of her that most identified her purpose for living.

She was a firefighter. She climbed ladders and drove large, noisy trucks. She wore several pounds of gear and ran into buildings filled with smoke. That was her life. Being a firefighter was who she was.

She looked at him and studied his profile in the moonlight. He was handsome, and charming, and fun. She liked him, and she was not sure she was ready yet to scare him away from her. Maybe one day, when they were good friends, he would be able to accept *all* of her, even the unconventional and, possibly, the most unattractive parts of her life. In the meantime, she wanted to enjoy his company and his teasing smile. She liked the way he made her heart flutter when he came near her. Sighing, she shook her head. "I was a clown once, with purple hair and a red sponge nose, for a Sisterhood celebration that Allison planned."

He chuckled and reached out to brush aside a wavy strand of hair that had blown across her forehead. "Why does that not surprise me, Delaney?"

She cleared her throat as she realized that he was still touching her cheek with his fingertips. "How did you guess that I was pantomiming *Cinderella*?"

"What?"

She swallowed as her skin burned under his fingertips. "I just wondered how you knew the right fairytale last night."

His dark blue eyes sparkled in the moonlight. Delaney studied his distinctive facial features. His high, chiseled cheeks bones; long, thin nose; and narrow face held the look of intelligence and compassion; but her eyes were continually drawn to his mouth—that wonderful, perfect, kissable mouth.

She blinked when she heard him chuckle. Wow! Climbing up to the top floor of the Driftwood Grill had not turned out to be such a good idea.

"I have two young nieces. They adore fairy tales and princesses and happy-ever-after stories." His fingers moved from her face to the hollow of her neck just above the knitted edge of her collarless shirt. A trail of heat marked where he had touched—and yet, she shivered. "Are you cold?"

As if in slow motion, she shook her head. "You read fairy tales to your nieces?"

He slid his hand under her hair and caressed the back of her neck. "When Lucie and Lizzie were younger, they had picture books filled with castles, and dragons, and beautiful princesses. Now they have a big anthology of fairy tales from around the world and dozens of animated cartoon movies filled with fantasy adventures that we have to watch every weekend. I think I know most of the dialogue and song lyrics by heart."

Delaney smiled. "That's so nice."

Gareth Collins seemed too good to be true. If he didn't stop touching her nape with his gentle fingertips, she was going to fall into his arms and beg him to kiss her.

"I'm afraid I'm a real sap when it comes to fairy-tale endings. I actually look forward to the part when the guy gets the girl and they live happily ever after."

His mouth was so close to hers that she could feel the warmth of his breath on her lips. She inhaled a long, deep breath, and his musky, masculine scent made her dizzy. Swallowing, she edged a step away from him. He was going to kiss her, and that prospect overwhelmed her. Not only did the idea scare her, but so did her acknowledgement that she truly wanted it to happen.

She breathed in balmy sea air and took another step away from him. Sighing, she looked up at the sky filled with bright, twinkling stars. "Oh, I wish the sun was out right now." She turned in the direction of the sound of waves rushing onto the nearby beach. "I've always loved to see the Atlantic Ocean and Pamlico Sound from the same spot." She folded her arms around her waist and turned in the opposite direction. "I enjoy the feeling of seeing water all around me and realizing I'm standing on this tiny strip of land that is so vulnerable to tropical storms, and hurricanes, and the day-to-day ebb and flow of the tides."

She gazed up at the sky as she made a complete circle with her body. "I feel so small and insignificant up here, as though some powerful force is controlling my life. It's not a negative power but more like an order that just makes sense. It's something that's taking care of things so I don't have to worry. I can just sit back and relax. I can finally enjoy the ride."

Delaney sensed Gareth approaching her, but he didn't attempt to touch her again. Relief mixed with disappointment. She wasn't at all sure what she wanted from him.

"I know that I haven't seen you under the best of circumstances, Delaney. Waking up you and your cat, and then startling you during the hula dance and causing you to fall were less-than-ideal situations in which to judge a person's emotional state, but, even compared to those awkward things, I can't help but think that you appear to be bothered by something."

When she pulled her gaze from the night sky to look at him, his eyes were already on her. "I suppose it goes without saying that I've been completely embarrassed."

He smiled. "I understand. I caught you off guard in both instances, and you didn't have time to throw up your defenses."

"My defenses?"

"You know—your mask that assures everyone that things are okay with you, that you have no concerns, and that you're not hurting inside."

Delaney stared at him. What was he doing? "Nothing is bothering me. I'm on vacation."

He nodded. "Yes, you're on vacation. You're going through the motions. You're trying to pretend you're relaxing and enjoying yourself."

Her chest tightened. The truth of his words was making her uncomfortable. "I *am* enjoying myself."

He set a hand on her shoulders. "I'm not trying to pry, Delaney."

"There's nothing for you to pry into. You don't know me."

He massaged her shoulder with his fingers. "I get the sense that something's upset you so much that you've come to Hatteras Island to forget, something that's made you very unhappy."

She shook her head. "No."

"Now, up here, close to the stars, you seem very relaxed. It's been wonderful to watch the transformation."

She swallowed as his fingers moved in gentle movements along the taut cord of her neck. His feather-light touch sent her pulse racing and warmed every part of her body.

His voice was close to her ear as he spoke. "I think this island is good for you. It gives you peace."

In the light of the moon, Delaney turned her head to study the man who had accompanied her to the top of the world. She inhaled the humid ocean air and filled her lungs with a slow, soothing breath. "I really love Hatteras. Summer just wouldn't be the same without staying at the beach."

He dropped his hand but continued to stand just inches from her at the railing overlooking Pamlico Sound. "You come to the Outer Banks often?"

She nodded. "The Suttons have been staying at the family beach house here in Avon since before I was born. It's as much a family tradition as caroling on Christmas Eve."

"Like the Sutton Sisterhood Sojourn."

"Yes, exactly."

"I like the idea of keeping time-honored customs in a family. I think tradition provides a sense of stability and security in a world full of constant change."

She glanced at him as he looked in the direction of the waters of the sound. "So philosophical. Does the Collins family have any particularly interesting customs?"

"We have a few special ones for Christmas, but not for summers on the Outer Banks. We live here."

"All of you? Really?"

"My parents have a house in Kitty Hawk. Nate and his family live here in Avon. I have a little bungalow next to my brother's house south of the village where I usually stay when I'm not in Richmond."

"Richmond? Do you have a plumbing business there?"

His chuckle rolled through the night air and made her heart skip a beat. She wondered what was so funny.

"My father and Nate are the real plumbers in our family."

"You fixed our washer."

He nodded. "I know only the basics. As I told you, I'm just filling in while Nate's recovering." He chuckled again. "The Sutton sisters were lucky that their washer required only simple repairs. If I encounter anything too complicated, I have to defer the problem to my father. I'm afraid I didn't inherit the skills for such a profession."

"So, what skills did you inherit?"

The question was out before Delaney thought about the consequences. If she delved too deeply into Gareth's personal life, he would have every right to demand the same from her.

She held her breath in the refreshing ocean air and waited for his response. Racing thoughts tumbled through her mind as she tried to think of a way to answer his own questions about her work, if he decided to ask.

"On the assumption that I have inherited marketable skills, I guess I could say that I'm a careful driver and fairly competent in the kitchen. I can grow tomatoes and sweet green peppers in a plastic bucket on the porch and construct a three-story castle out of sand."

The sound and spontaneity of her laughter surprised

her. It had been a long time since humor had sparked her wounded spirit.

"I didn't realize I was being humorous." The outside edges of his mouth tugged as though he was trying not to smile. He looked down at her with penetrating blue eyes and a warm, accepting expression.

"Given the opportunity to brag about themselves, nearly all people tend to boast about their most prestigious professional accomplishments. They don't usually talk about growing tomatoes and building sand castles. You must have experienced some success in your life that's made you proud."

"I suppose I consider myself to be a good listener." Holding her gaze, he laced his fingers with hers and gave her hand a gentle squeeze. "I can be a good listener, Delaney."

Hal Barker, her friend and colleague, had been a good listener. Maybe that was the one thing she missed most about Hal now that he was gone. She missed talking with him.

"I can keep a confidence too. You can trust me with your secrets."

"I don't have any secrets." Her voice was almost a whisper.

He squeezed her hand again and then folded her fingers in his palm. "Everyone has secrets, but I respect your right to privacy. Just know that I'm here, if ever you need a good listener."

The familiar sense of sadness and loss began inching its way into her heart. Not only had she lost a friend in that explosion over a year before, but she had somehow lost her will to recover from the endless destruction and hurt she observed every day as a professional fire-fighter. Maybe Chief Adler was right. Perhaps she was no longer able to face the challenges of such a demanding career.

Her head began to spin, and she closed her eyes as she remembered that awful day. Noise of the fire roared through the abandoned warehouse. A dizzy feeling made her legs unsteady, and she trembled, too afraid to move, too afraid to breathe. Nausea filled her stomach.

Heat and smoke were everywhere. She lost sight of Hal Barker as his tall frame disappeared into the hallway. She tried to orient herself in the gloom and shadows. Then a powerful blow knocked her to the floor, and everything, including her memory of that horrendous moment, went dark.

"Are you all right?"

She opened her eyes as she felt the firm support of muscular arms around her waist. She felt a strong heart beat a regular and comforting rhythm as she lifted her head from his chest.

"What happened, Delaney?"

Swallowing, she tried to focus her thoughts. "Just a little lightheaded, I guess."

"Here. Sit down." He guided her to a nearby bench.

Her legs wobbled so much that she was sure she

would have fallen right over the railing on the roof of the Driftwood Grill if Gareth hadn't stopped her. He sat down beside her on the narrow wooden seat.

When she looked up into his deep blue eyes, obvious concern filled his face, and he smiled at her. She inhaled slow, steady breaths in an attempt to calm her racing heart and to alleviate the uneasiness that always overwhelmed her whenever she remembered the explosion that had knocked her unconscious and killed her fellow firefighter.

Gareth reached out and brushed his fingertips along her cheek. "Okay now?"

She nodded and forced a smile. "I'm fine." She rose to her feet. "We'd better get back down there before my sisters start to worry."

He stood beside her and slid an arm around her waist. "I'm already worried about you, Delaney."

"I'm okay. Really."

He caught her arm as she headed toward the ladder leading to the ground. "I don't think that's a good idea."

"I'm serious, Gareth. You don't know the Sutton sisters."

"No, I mean, you shouldn't take the ladder. It's not safe for you to climb that distance when you've been experiencing dizziness."

He gave her forearm a squeeze. "Let's check the stairs. The paint is probably dry already anyway."

She studied him for a moment in the moonlight. Then she nodded. "All right. We'll take the stairs."

He slipped his hand over hers. "Come on. Let's go find your sisters."

"Okay, let's have it, Del."

"We want the details."

"And you can't use the excuse that you're too tired, Delaney. It's already ten o'clock."

Delaney smoothed her palm over the soft, smooth fur of Max's back and glanced around the wicker table on the second-floor balcony at the three pairs of gray eyes looking back at her. She hadn't slept most of the night. Tossing and turning, she'd dreamed the same dream over and over again. She had fought countless blazes and rescued numerous firefighters; and every time she'd removed the headgear and mask of an injured colleague, Gareth Collins was smiling up at her.

Cassie, of course, had slept soundly through the night. After Delaney and Gareth had returned to their table inside the Driftwood Grill, Brianna had feigned tiredness and said that she wanted to go back to the beach house. Delaney had suspected that her sisters simply wanted to hear about everything that had happened between her and Gareth, but she'd insisted on going straight to bed.

Cassie had followed her, but, to Delaney's relief, she hadn't pressed her for details. Her older sister had fallen asleep almost instantly, and Delaney had laid awake reliving the moments she had spent with Gareth Collins on the roof of the Driftwood Grill.

But now it's morning, and I have to tell them some-

thing. If I don't, I won't have a peaceful moment all day. Delaney stroked Max's back again and rubbed his ears as the feline snuggled into her lap.

"Come on, Del."

"We're dying of curiosity here."

"We need to know *everything*."

Delaney sighed. "There's nothing to tell, really."

Cassie threw up her hands into the warm summer air. "You're going to have to do better than that."

Brianna buttered a fresh-baked banana muffin and then licked her fingers as she nodded. "Spill it, Delaney. We've been waiting with unbelievable patience. You owe us some juicy information about you and Gareth up on that roof."

"Did he kiss you?"

Allison's quiet question caught her by surprise, and she stared across the table at her oldest sister who was slicing a large, ripe cantaloupe. She watched Allison scoop seeds and pulp from the center of the fruit with a spoon and then pick up the knife again. "Melon, Delaney?"

She shook her head. Nausea twisted in her stomach, and her head was throbbing. Food did not appeal to her, and she was not in the mood to answer a barrage of questions just to satisfy her sisters' overactive imaginations. She had been restless the entire night. Her eyes were scratchy and unfocused. Her whole body felt tired and full of nervous tension.

"Well, did he?"

"Did he what, Cassie?"

"Did Gareth kiss you when you were up on the roof?"

"I think that's so romantic." Brianna took the slice of cantaloupe Allison held out to her. "Up there so high with the stars and the moon all around you."

It was romantic, at least, until I made a fool of myself and almost collapsed in his arms. What a complete embarrassment! He must think I'm the biggest idiot on Hatteras Island.

"We're waiting."

Cassie narrowed her eyes at Delaney as Allison and Brianna also turned to her. "Spill it, Del."

"No." She shifted in her chair, and Max stretched and gave her a don't-you-see-I'm-trying-to-sleep-here look. "Gareth didn't kiss me."

"But he wanted to, right?" Brianna wiped melon juice from her chin with a paper napkin. "I could tell when he was sitting at the table with us that he wanted to kiss you."

Allison smiled at her. "He likes you, Delaney."

Cassie nodded and took a banana muffin from the cloth lined basket in the center of the table. "He's crazy about you. He just might not know it yet."

"Oh, he knows it." Brianna reached for another slice of cantaloupe. "The way he looked at you last night told me that."

Allison nodded. "I think Gareth is a very cautious man, especially when it comes to his emotions. I'm sure he moves into relationships with slow deliberation."

Delaney twirled the end of Max's tail around her finger. "Do you mind if we talk about something else?"

"Yes, we do mind."

The words Cassie and Brianna spoke in unison hung in the air for a split second before the two sisters laughed. They raised their right hands and slapped palms above the table.

Allison smiled. "We are really getting in-sync with each other. By the end of the weekend, we won't even have to speak. We'll all just be reading each other's minds."

Delaney groaned as she considered going back to bed. Max was already dozing on her lap.

"Come on, Del. Tell us more."

"We want to hear everything."

"There's nothing more. We climbed to the roof. We looked at the stars. We climbed back down."

"There must be something else, Del."

"He told me his family actually lives here on the Outer Banks."

Cassie grinned. "Really? Now, isn't that interesting? A native."

"Gareth stays here in the summer, but he has a place in Richmond too."

"He's a plumber in Richmond?"

Delaney shook her head. "He must do something else." She recalled their conversation about his lack of plumbing skills and other interests. *Good cook. Good grower of vegetables. Good listener. Good builder of sand castles.*

She smiled at the last one as she tried to imagine him kneeling on the beach while his strong hands created moats, and keeps, and towers out of piles of fine white Hatteras Island sand. Those hands were so wonderful when they smoothed out tension and offered comfort. Maybe Gareth Collins was a massage therapist.

Cassie grinned. "I found out about one of his interests here on the Outer Banks."

Delaney set one hand on Max's back and felt his rhythmic breathing as he napped with obvious contentment. The grin on her sister's face made her cringe. *Now what?*

"I bet he's a pilot." Brianna poured a tall glass of orange juice from a carafe. "He has his own plane, doesn't he?"

Allison shook her head. "No, I think he's in some kind of health-care profession, a nurse, maybe, or a physical therapist."

Cassie's smile broadened. "While Del and he were kissing on the top level of the Driftwood Grill, I had a little talk with a couple that knows Gareth."

"We were not kissing."

Cassie nodded. "Their names are Barry and Nancy Granger. They live here in Avon and are friends of Gareth's brother Nate."

Brianna finished her juice. "So, what did the Grangers tell you?"

"They've known the whole Collins family a long time." Cassie's gray eyes sparkled. "It happens that Barry has been spending quite a bit of time with Gareth because they're both members of the volunteer fire department here."

Cassie slapped Delaney's back. "Isn't that great? You both wear uniforms and drive big trucks. How romantic is that?"

Delaney shook her head at the realization that her sister could reduce her profession to the brief, six-word description of *wear uniforms and drive big trucks.* What was even more frustrating to Delaney than her sister's remark was the knowledge that most people she knew agreed with Cassie's simplistic view of her job. She wondered if anyone besides fellow firefighters, and perhaps their spouses, truly understood the emotional and mental toll such a career took on an individual's life.

Until that horrible day when the fire had killed Hal Barker and left Delaney full of doubts, she'd never questioned her choice of work. Now, it seemed, she wondered about it most of the time. Was firefighting worth all of the pain, and effort, and anxiety? Was she still committed to that particular challenge? Chief Adler didn't think so. Sometimes Delaney was not sure.

"Well, there you go." Brianna broke some green grapes off a bunch on a plate in front of her. "At least you know you have something in common to talk about."

Delaney shook her head. "I'm not sure the fact that we're both firefighters is going to help."

Cassie shook her head. "Why not?"

Brianna narrowed her eyes. "I really don't see what all the fuss is about."

Allison poured coffee from a thermal pitcher. "I think

what Delaney is trying to say is that Gareth's being a firefighter himself brings specific difficulties to the development of a serious relationship because he has first-hand knowledge of the dangers of such an occupation."

"Right." Delaney nodded, but she knew that the real trouble was not Gareth's choice of volunteer work. What really bothered her was the idea that she was starting to have feelings for him.

"I didn't say that a relationship was impossible, though." Allison's gray eyes leveled on Delaney's from across the table.

A warm breeze blew from the ocean and fluttered the edges of the cloth covering the table. It felt refreshing on Delaney's bare arms and neck. She wished the breakfast conversation would turn to a subject that didn't involve her social life.

Of course, a relationship with Gareth was possible—but did she want that complication in her life at this point? She smoothed her right palm over Max's soft fur. A relationship with any man, especially a volunteer firefighter, would take much more time and energy than she could probably give. On the other hand, forgetting Gareth Collins wouldn't be easy. Especially that kissable mouth.

His deep blue eyes and warm smile flashed through her mind. She imagined again the gentle touch of his hands on her shoulders. Yes, ridding her mind of thoughts of Gareth Collins would definitely be difficult, if that was what she wanted.

With a long sigh, she scooped Max into her arms and rose to her feet. "I'm going to take a shower."

She opened the glass door leading to the kitchen and stepped into the cool air-conditioned room. She didn't realize that someone had followed her until she heard Brianna's voice.

"Wait, Delaney."

When she turned, she was surprised to find her sister walking across the ceramic floor. Her rubber-soled sandals made a soft clapping sound as she held one arm around her abdomen.

In an instant, she rushed to Brianna's side. "Is it the baby? What's wrong?"

Brianna shook her head as she reached for the back of a stool at the counter separating the eating area from the sink and appliances. "No, I'm fine. I was just wondering if you would mind helping me go shopping for dinner tonight. Allison said we could choose a partner."

She rubbed the cotton shirt stretching over her front. "I'm not in the best of shape to run around town getting the supplies I'll need for a Cape Cod clambake."

Delaney smiled as she shifted the still-sleeping Max to her right arm and slid her left one around Brianna's shoulders. "A clambake. Yummy. Sure, I'll help. Just give me a few minutes to get ready."

"Thanks again for helping out with the shopping, Delaney. I think we have all the ingredients we need to make the fried clams and corn chowder."

As Delaney pushed the grocery cart piled high with food along the supermarket aisle, she glanced over at the list Brianna held. She struggled to keep the heavy cart on a straight course as her sister crossed off items on the piece of paper in her hand.

"We must have almost everything else too. It looks like we're getting enough to feed a small army. After all, there are only four of us."

Brianna grinned and patted her stomach. "Five. This baby is always hungry. "Don't forget that we have to stop at that little seafood shop near the pier on our way home. I'm going to get some lobsters to steam."

Brianna walked a few more steps. "Oh, I think I should go back and get some cranberry juice. There's a special fruit punch I want to make. We'll have to return to the third aisle—or was it the fourth?" Her sister shrugged. "Anyway, it's toward the beginning, at the other side of the store. Uh, oh—"

Concentrating on maneuvering the grocery cart around a display of glass bottles of barbecue sauce and pickles, Delaney glanced at Brianna. "Did we forget something else?"

"No. At least, I don't think so." Brianna shook her head as she nudged her elbow into Delaney's side. "Look—over there, next to the bakery counter. Oh, no—don't look. Isn't that Gareth?"

Chapter Five

Without thinking, Delaney turned to look in the direction Brianna had indicated and nearly steered the heavy grocery cart into a pyramid display of plastic ketchup and mustard containers. With a sharp left twist, she missed the tower by less than an inch.

"I can see only his back, but as Cassie has pointed out to us, he looks rather appealing from that angle as well, and—"

"Brianna!" Delaney whispered her sister's name between clenched teeth. "Please."

"Well, it's Gareth, isn't it? There, he's turning so you can see his profile. Yes, I'm right. Let's go say hi."

"No. Come on, Brianna." Delaney struggled to push the cart toward the check-out counters near the entrance of the store. "We need to get all of this food back to the house."

Her persistent sister ignored her, of course, and she heard Brianna's friendly voice call out, "Well, good morning, Gareth. What a pleasant surprise."

Delaney rolled her eyes and pushed their heavy cart to follow her. She gave Gareth a reluctant wave with her hand when he smiled in her direction.

"Hello, ladies. It looks as though you're really stocking up on supplies for the week."

Brianna shook her head. "Most of it's for tonight. It's my turn to cook." She grinned. "We're having a Cape Cod clambake."

Dark brows rose a quarter of an inch above his expressive blue eyes. "Another sisterhood celebration?"

Brianna nodded. "Yes, foods from the Cape Cod area. I thought that, since the Mayflower landed near there, we'd dress up like Pilgrims, all prim and proper with bonnets and white collars. Delaney has agreed to be Squanto and to perform a traditional Native American dance before we eat."

"I have not. I told you I'd help you shop, but I'm not dancing—never."

Her sister smiled. "Sure you will. We'll have a good time."

Delaney sighed in frustration as she watched Gareth grin in apparent amusement. *Oh, what you must think of our family.*

"I have a little suede skirt and vest with beads and fringe for you. I even found a pair of moccasins. You'll look very authentic."

"Authentic Native American, with wavy blond hair and gray eyes." Delaney shook her head in irritation as she noted the amused expression on Gareth's face. "Really authentic, Brianna."

Her sister shrugged. "Maybe not, but it'll be fun."

She glanced at the full cart of groceries. "We should probably get this food home."

Brianna reached out and touched Gareth's arm. "Would you like to come over for a while and visit? We'd love to have you join us for a lazy Sunday afternoon. We'll tell you stories about our summers on Hatteras Island."

Oh, no. Come on, Brianna. No more embarrassing comments, please.

His dark brows lifted a fraction of an inch again. "I thought only Sutton sisters were allowed at Sutton Sisterhood celebrations."

"Oh, they are. That's a rule Allison firmly established right when we first started." Brianna's eyes sparkled as she continued her explanation. "It has to be that way, you know. If we allowed one or two outsiders to join us at our retreats, then some of us might be less inclined to talk openly and share certain thoughts and feelings." She turned her gaze to Delaney for a moment before looking back at Gareth. "Even other family members aren't allowed—parents, husbands, children. Everyone has to stay away during our designated evenings together. Sisters have a special bond, you know."

Gareth shook his head. "I'm not sure I do, but I'm trying to understand."

She reached out and touched his arm. "We prepare with elaborate themes, and play silly games, and maybe embarrass ourselves a bit."

Maybe? Delaney inhaled a long, steady breath and wished she could hurry her talkative, overly friendly sister toward a check-out line.

"But we have a wonderful time reuniting with each other after a busy year of living and working in different places and being separated the whole time except for telephone calls, and e-mails, and short visits for holidays. Our motto is—"

"Relax. Rejuvenate. Reconnect." Gareth winked at Delaney.

Her heart thudded against her chest, and she swallowed. Had she noticed before how blue and intense his eyes were? And that smile. It could take away her breath if she wasn't careful.

"Yes, the Sutton Sisterhood motto. Delaney mentioned it."

Brianna bobbed her head up and down. "And we take it very seriously. So this evening at six o'clock we'll begin our clambake. No one else is invited to join us, but there is absolutely no rule about our having company before six."

Delaney watched her sister give Gareth a long look. Oh, if only she could think of something to say to stop Brianna from continuing the conversation.

"Why don't you stop by for a while this afternoon? Delaney and I have just one more stop to make, and then we're heading back to the beach house."

He smiled, and Delaney's heart soared. *Wow!* She could not recall a man who had ever affected her senses with such intensity as Gareth Collins did with a simple smile. Well, she could hardly call it simple. His smile seemed to light up his face and give his expression a joyous quality. His chiseled cheekbones rose as little lines crinkled and fanned out from the corners of his dancing blue eyes.

She inhaled a deep breath,, and her head filled with the subtle scent of soap and woodsy aftershave. *Uh-oh.* She and Brianna needed to get to a check-out *soon.*

"I appreciate the invitation, but I actually have other plans for this afternoon. I promised my nieces that I'd take them to the beach as soon as I finished my shopping."

He smiled again, and Delaney's heart jumped again. With reluctance, she pulled her eyes from his face. She repeated the question that continued to confuse her: Why was a simple social gesture wreaking such havoc on her body? Maybe she was getting sick. Maybe she was coming down with some kind of summertime cold or stomach virus. Maybe there was an unknown disease that affected the beat and rhythm of one's heart at the sight of someone else smiling. Delaney inhaled another deep breath. *Yes, that's it. I'm getting sick.*

"Delaney?"

She felt a hand on her arm. Seeing Brianna's questioning gray eyes studying her, she swallowed. The lump in her throat was bigger than a golf ball.

"What's wrong, Delaney?"

"Nothing." She shook her head. "Nothing's wrong. Why?"

She felt Gareth's gaze on her too. "Would you consider accompanying my nieces and me to the beach this afternoon, Delaney? We'll be back in plenty of time for you to dress in your suede skirt and moccasins for your Cape Cod celebration."

"A Sunday at the beach. How nice." Brianna's gray eyes sparkled.

She patted Delaney's arm. "Come on. We have to get going."

"Wait. Will you come with me?"

Brianna grinned. "Oh, she'll be happy to accept your invitation, won't you, Delaney? What time will you be picking her up?"

Gareth glanced at his watch and then met Delaney's eyes. "About an hour from now? Will that be time enough for you?"

Brianna nodded. "That will be just fine."

"Delaney?"

He waited for her to answer. She gazed into his deep blue eyes and felt as though she were floating in a huge pool of emotion. Going to the beach with Gareth Collins was *not* a good idea.

"An hour, yes. That will be plenty of time."

"Is that what you're wearing?"

Delaney combed her hair with her fingers and then pulled it all to the back of her neck with an elastic band. Setting a canvas Baltimore Orioles cap on her head, she looped the ponytail through the hole in the back and turned toward the open bedroom door.

All of her sisters stood in the hallway watching her. Delaney leaned down to retrieve a pair of rubber flip flops from under her bed.

"You can't wear those cut-off jeans over your swim suit," Allison said.

She slid her left foot into one flip flop. "Why not?"

"You've had them since you were sixteen."

"You wore the jeans until they were paper-thin, and then you cut them off for shorts."

"Don't you have a nice skirt or something?"

Delaney stared at her sisters. "We're going to the beach."

Allison stepped into the room and slipped her arm around Delaney's shoulders. "This is your first date with the one who will someday be your husband and the love of your life. Gareth is the man of your dreams."

My husband? The love of my life? Man of my dreams? Had Allison guessed that the waves of her subconscious thought had drifted from the unknown, nebulous form to the face of Gareth Collins whenever she dreamed of rescuing a fellow firefighter? *No.* Allison could not possibly know. Delaney had never shared the subject of her nightly hauntings, the scenes that plagued her whenever she tried to sleep. The fact that her dream had taken a certain ironic and, perhaps, amusing twist after her having met Gareth on Hatteras Island did little to comfort her.

"Don't you have something more feminine than ten-year-old shorts and a faded tee shirt with an unrecognizable picture of the Ocracoke lighthouse on the front?"

Delaney looked down at the pale yellow shirt she was wearing over her swim suit. "If it's so unrecognizable, then how do you know it's a picture of the Ocracoke light?"

Cassie rolled her eyes. "We've seen you in it only about a million times since you bought it how many years ago? Seven? Eight? It was the summer after Allison and Zach got married. I remember because we all took the ferry over to Ocracoke Island for a bicycle ride around the village. You found that shirt in a little shop next to the ice cream place where we all got hot fudge sundaes and iced teas."

"Okay, so you have an infallible memory." Delaney shrugged. "The point is that I'm going to the beach. Why should I dress up to get splashed with salt water and covered with sand?"

Brianna grasped her hand. "Gareth needs to see your very best qualities, and dressing like a tomboy is not going to spark the romantic flame we're hoping to ignite."

"Romantic flame? With his two nieces?"

Allison squeezed her shoulders. "Don't under-estimate the power of a flattering dress on even the most distracted man. Gareth may be watching his brother's children, but his attention will be on you."

Delaney shook her head and slipped her right foot into the other flip flop. "I'm wearing what I have on. There's the doorbell. It's probably Gareth."

"We could keep him company till you change."

"Put on your green gauze skirt and the blouse with the hibiscus flowers."

"And your espadrilles with the lace up ribbons that tie around your ankles."

Delaney pulled away from her sisters and grabbed a lightweight cotton cardigan draped across the back of a nearby chair. "I don't wear skirts to the beach." She leaned over the bed to smooth Max's fur as he lay napping next to her pillow. "Take care of things while I'm gone, Champ. Make sure these crazy sisters of mine have a nice Sunday afternoon."

Gareth parked his car in the Collins family driveway. After introducing Delaney to Lucie, who was eight, and to Lizzie, who was six, they all headed to the nearby boardwalk built to protect the delicate dunes from the constant foot traffic of humans visiting the beach each day.

Lucie carried a small umbrella, and Lizzie swung a plastic pail and shovel from her arm. Gareth had a small insulated bag slung over one shoulder and a towel draped around his neck.

In faded khaki shorts and a worn tee shirt, Gareth appeared relaxed and comfortable. The girls, too, had on worn shorts and cotton tops over their swim suits, and baseball caps to shade their heads from the heat of the afternoon sun. Despite her sisters' doubts, Delaney was confident that she was dressed in appropriate attire. She followed the little group onto the huge expanse of white sand and inhaled a long breath of salty summer air.

First they strolled barefoot along the water's edge while the girls picked up pieces of shells and looked for jellyfish. Then they made footprints in the wet sand and watched the surf wash them away again.

Gareth passed out bottles of juice, and they all sat together in the shade of the umbrella while seagulls swooped in the clear sky above and sand pipers skittered near the incoming waves. As the girls tossed pieces of dry bread to the birds, Delaney enjoyed the heat of the afternoon sun tempered by the continual sea breeze.

"Let's build a castle, Uncle Gareth!" Lucie ran toward the umbrella under which Delaney sat as Gareth munched a green apple next to her. "A big one with lots of towers and a high wall all around it to keep the princess safe." The tall, lanky girl skidded to a stop just inches from the edge of the large terrycloth towel. Light grains from the beach sprayed in the direction of the umbrella and covered the towel and their clothing with a layer of fine, white sand.

"Lucie!" Gareth sent Delaney a look of obvious apology as he reached over and brushed grit from her bare knees. "Be careful."

His brown-haired niece grinned as she readjusted her pale blue baseball cap. "Sorry."

"Hey, let's build a castle now!" Following her sister up from the surf, Lizzie rushed toward them and sent sand in every direction. "I can get water for the moat with my pail."

Gareth shook his head and shrugged as he handed Delaney another towel. "I guess some members of the Collins family need to work on their beach etiquette."

She wiped sand from her eyes and smiled. "You haven't met the rest of the Sutton family yet. My nieces and sisters believe that the more sand one takes back after a day at the beach, the better."

Gareth's chuckle rumbled from somewhere deep inside him. "Having met the Sutton sisters, I believe you without question. The fact that beach sand doesn't bother them does not surprise me at all." He met her eyes. "But you, Delaney Sutton, amaze me a good deal."

Amaze you? What does that mean?

Lizzie pulled on his arm. "Come on, Uncle Gareth. Let's make a beautiful home for a princess. Will you help us, Delaney?"

True to his word, Gareth Collins, with the assistance

of his two nieces, constructed an incredible castle of sand on the beach on Hatteras Island. Delaney watched in astonishment as the man who had repaired the washer in her family's beach house instructed the two little girls in the intricacies of building drawbridges, turrets, keeps, dungeons, and moats. The whole process took more than an hour and enormous amounts of sand. When the project was complete, the castle was several feet long and as high as Delaney's waist.

At Lizzie's insistence, Gareth propped a camera on the cooler and a pile of towels while Delaney squatted next to his nieces in front of the castle. Activating the self-timer button, he rushed to kneel close to Delaney before the camera snapped a photograph of the multi-story structure and its creators.

"Let's go wash our hands in the waves and then have some juice!" Lizzie bounced up and down sending sand in every direction.

Lucie and Lizzie squealed as they ran toward the water and jumped over the incoming waves. The two little girls splashed in the water and skipped across the wet sand.

"They seem to have forgotten that they're thirsty."

Gareth slipped a pair of sunglasses onto his face as he watched his nieces frolic at the water's edge. "I suppose you know how easily children are distracted."

Delaney grinned up at him. "It's been my experience that playing in the ocean can distract a person from some of the most distressing circumstances of life."

He looked down at her and studied her with such intensity that her heart skipped a beat. A part of her wanted to pull away her gaze, but another part continued to meet his deep blue eyes and to sink into a pool of indescribable emotions.

He lifted his right hand and brushed his fingertips across her cheek. "I hope some day you'll feel comfortable enough to share some of those distressing circumstances with me."

She cleared her throat. "What makes you think I was talking about me?"

He set his fingers on her chin. "I sense a connection between us. Am I wrong?"

She moistened her lips with the tip of her tongue. "About a connection between us, or about suffering from potentially distressing circumstances?"

He leaned so close to her that she felt the heat of his breath fan across her cheek. "Someday, Delaney, you will trust me enough to unburden yourself."

"I have no burdens."

"Denying them doesn't make them go away."

"Are we going to get something to drink, Uncle Gareth?" Lucie caught his left hand and pulled him toward the umbrella and cooler. "Let's go have some juice." The little girl turned in the direction of the water once again. "Come on, Lizzie. Hurry! I'm thirsty."

The younger child waved and began to run, but as soon as she took a few steps, she screamed and fell onto the wet sand. "Oh, my foot!" Lizzie clutched her left foot and cried out in obvious pain as she rocked back and forth. "Ouch, Uncle Gareth—something hurts a lot." Tears streamed down her face as her uncle rushed to her and kneeled down beside her. He tried to brush wet sand from the bottom of the child's foot as she squealed and attempted to pull away from him.

"What happened, Lizzie?" Lucie squatted in the sand next to her sister. "Did you step on a jellyfish? Did it sting you?"

"I don't know. Oh, Uncle Gareth, it hurts so much."

The older child turned to her uncle. "Did Lizzie get stung?"

Gareth shook his head. "I can't see." He lifted Lizzie into his arms as a strong wave rushed toward them. "I'm going to dip you into the water to rinse the sand off the bottom of your foot, honey."

Lizzie screamed when he bent his legs and lowered his niece's foot toward the water. She flung her arms around his neck and buried her face against his shoulder. He carried her up the beach and set her on the towel in the shade of the umbrella.

"Did something bite her, Uncle Gareth?" Lucie asked as she and Delaney followed them.

Gareth shook his head as he examined the bottom of Lizzie's foot. "I think your sister probably stepped on a broken sea shell."

Lucie kneeled in the sand next to the other little girl and studied the sole of Lizzie's foot. "I don't see anything."

"Well, it hurts really badly. Is it bleeding, Uncle Gareth?"

He glanced up at Delaney and then shook his head. "I don't even see a mark, honey. I'm sure you foot hurts now, but I think you're going to be all right."

Lizzie sniffed. "I will?"

He nodded. "I'm positive."

The little girl sighed. "I think I need a hug."

"You do?"

"Yes, I'm sure I'll feel better after a hug from you."

Gareth sat down on the blanket beside Lizzie and held out his arms. His niece fell into them, and he hugged her for several seconds and rubbed his palms up and down her back.

Finally Lizzie raised her head and looked at him. "I always feel better after we hug, Uncle Gareth."

He smiled down at her. "That's what hugging's for, to help make us all feel better."

Lizzie lifted her cap from her head and brushed hair from her eyes before replacing the hat. "Do your kids want hugs when they get hurt or feel sad?"

Your kids? Delaney wondered what the child's question meant. Did Gareth have a family somewhere that he hadn't mentioned?

"Usually they don't want hugs."

"Why not?"

"They're big boys, and they think hugs are silly and won't help them feel better."

"Aren't hugs for grownup kids too?"

"Hugs are for everybody, Lizzie. They are the perfect way to tell people you care about them and hope they'll feel better some day."

Lucie leaned toward her uncle and sister. "Don't your kids like you to care about them?"

"Sometimes they're afraid. They think that if someone cares about them when they hurt, then it will hurt even more when the person stops caring."

"But you won't stop caring, will you, Uncle Gareth?"

"The boys I work with don't believe that. You see, Lucie, they've been hurt so many times that they don't trust people anymore."

"Will they ever trust others again?"

"Maybe one day after they talk and work through their problems and feelings. It takes a long time to learn to trust after a person has stopped trusting."

Sighing, Gareth rose to his feet. "Come on. We should be getting back. Your mom will be wondering what's taking us so long."

The little group collected empty juice and water bottles and put everything back into the cooler. Lizzie picked up her plastic pail and shovel while Delaney helped Lucie shake sand out of the beach towels they had used.

Gareth pulled the umbrella from the sand before retracting the pole and then winding the nylon material and plastic frame around it. He snapped the straps to secure the closed umbrella in place and handed it to his older niece. "Are we all set?"

"I'm still thirsty," Lucie said.

"Me too, Uncle Gareth."

Delaney scanned the area of beach where they'd been sitting. The only evidence of their presence there was the flattened imprint of a towel and the elaborate castle that would be completely washed away by the waters of the next high tide.

"We'll have something to drink when we get home."

Lizzie shrugged. "I guess we have everything then."

Lucie slipped her hand into Delaney's. "I'm glad you could come with us. It was really fun. Uncle Gareth doesn't usually invite his friends to come to the beach on Sundays with us."

Delaney glanced at the tall man who was busy adjusting the long handle of the cooler over his shoulder while balancing a pile of beach towels against his arms. Smiling, she turned to the brown-haired child beside her.

"I had a wonderful time, Lucie. Thank you for letting me join you."

"Maybe you can come again next week." Lizzie sprinted past them toward the nearby boardwalk. Her red pail swung back and forth from its handle looped at her elbow. "Uncle Gareth brings us every Sunday, except when it rains."

Delaney turned again and caught his gaze. "Every Sunday?"

He shrugged broad shoulders as a grin tugged at the corners of his mouth, the mouth she could not get off her mind, the mouth she wanted to kiss. *Kiss? There it is again. What is **wrong** with me?*

"I like the beach. Why stay here on Hatteras Island and then retreat indoors during my free time? My two agreeable little nieces give me the perfect reason to come to the beach often to play in the sand."

"And go swimming!" Lucie said.

"And build castles!" Lizzie called from the edge of the wooden path over the dunes.

"And look for shells and feed the sea gulls." Lucie squeezed Delaney's hand. "I think Hatteras Island is the most wonderful place in the world."

A wave of satisfaction and warmth spread over her at that moment. She realized that, during the time she'd been at the beach, she had forgotten her insecurities about her career choice, the overwhelming sadness that plagued her, and the troubling dreams and sleepless nights that left her restless and indecisive about her life.

"Isn't that where you live, Delaney?" Lucie pointed toward the Sutton family beach house. "Who are those people on the porch up there?"

"They're all waving." Lizzie spotted the individuals her sister had noticed. "Are they waving to us?"

"I think they're motioning for us to go up there with them. Who are they?"

Delaney groaned in silence as she watched her three older sisters beckoning Gareth and the children to climb the steps onto the second floor balcony off the kitchen where the Suttons were sitting in chairs around the wicker table and enjoying the late-Sunday sunshine. Was it impossible to hope that they would leave her alone without interfering or offering advice for one afternoon?

She sighed as she realized how exhausting avoiding her sisters was going to be. If she decided she wanted to pursue a relationship with Gareth Collins, would she have the emotional stamina to face the Sutton sisters' continual meddling in her personal life?

"They want us to go up there, Uncle Gareth." Lizzie bounced up and down on the boardwalk. "Can we run ahead?"

Gareth lifted his brows as Delaney glanced up at him. His right arm rested on the strap of the collapsible cooler slung over his shoulder while his left one held a pile of damp, sandy towels. His old 35mm camera dangled against his chest, and the brim of his faded canvas baseball cap tilted toward his left ear and gave him a boyish, casual appearance that reminded her of old friends she used to have and the carefree summer days she'd spent as an adolescent at the beach years ago.

She had very few worries back then. Life had been wonderful, idyllic.

"Could we go see them—please?" Lizzie tugged on her arm and dragged Delaney's thoughts back to the porch where her three sisters were beckoning.

"Soon they'll be preparing for their authentic Cape Cod clambake. Maybe you shouldn't bother the members of the sisterhood." Gareth's quiet comment sent her heart into a momentary erratic beat.

"The sisterhood?" Lucie asked, still holding onto Delaney's other hand. "What's that?"

She swallowed. "They're my sisters—my three caring, meddling sisters."

Lizzie pulled on her arm again. "You have *three* sisters?"

"Wow! Lizzie and I have only each other."

Consider yourselves lucky. Delaney sighed and forced a smile. "Most of the time it's wonderful having a big family, but sometimes having so many sisters is a little irritating." She tried to ignore the fact that Cassie was now standing at the railing of the porch waving both of her arms and calling to them.

"Do their names begin with *D* like Lizzie and Lucie begin with *L*?" Lizzie asked.

Watching the Sutton sisters out of the corner of her eyes, Delaney shook her head. "No, I'm the only *D*. My sisters' names begin with *A, B,* and *C.*"

Lizzie's brown eyes grew large and round. "Your sisters are the alphabet?"

She smiled down at the child. "I guess you could say that."

"Hey, that's right! I never realized it." Gareth's exclamation and subsequent chuckle sent a wave of feelings through Delaney that she found hard not to notice. She nodded as she pushed away thoughts of flinging her arms around him with his load of wet towels, sandy tee shirt, camera, and a cooler full of empty drink containers still in his arms.

"Allison, Brianna, Cassandra, Delaney—my parents always said they would have named the next Sutton child Eleanor if there had been another."

Lucie squeezed Delaney's hand. "Don't you have any brothers?"

"Not a single one."

Gareth chuckled again. "I'm not sure a Sutton boy would have survived the Sisterhood. Perhaps if he'd been the oldest, a brother may have had a chance, but as the youngest, I can't imagine—"

Delaney sighed. "You can't imagine Sutton sisters leaving the poor kid alone or letting him grow up. You can't imagine him having any kind of life on his own."

"Well, yes." The corners of his mouth curved into a charming grin. "Your words may be a bit harsh, but I don't think being a male sibling to the Sutton sisters would be easy for a man, even if he did possess an extraordinary amount of patience and understanding."

Delaney glanced again at the porch where all three of her sisters stood along the railing waving and calling their names. She felt Lizzie tugging on her arm again.

"Can we go meet Delaney's sisters?"

"Please, Uncle Gareth!"

"They always have fresh-squeezed juice or lemonade waiting, and the girls *are* thirsty." Delaney looked back at Gareth. "I'm sure they'd love to meet your nieces if it's all right with you."

Chapter Six

Gareth smiled and then shrugged. "Okay, then, as long as you think it's all right." He nodded to his nieces. "Go ahead, girls. Run up and say hi, but you can't stay long. Your mom will be worried that we're not back yet."

Squealing, Lucie and Lizzie hurried along the board-walk as they waved back at the three Sutton sisters. From where she stood looking toward the beach house, Delaney saw Cassie nodding and holding her thumb high in the air.

Now, what does that mean? It's going to be a long night at Brianna's Cape Cod clambake. Delaney shook her head. She had a strong suspicion that Native Americans and lobster would not be the only topics of conversation at the sisters' meeting that evening.

"Something wrong?"

106

Gareth's quiet question pulled her attention back to him, and she forced a smile. "Nothing more than the usual dilemma I have of trying to control my sisters' enthusiasm about prying into my life."

The smile he returned was warm and appealing. He readjusted the pile of damp towels in his arms. "Having a large, caring family can have some benefits, too, I've heard."

She nodded as skepticism filled her mind. "A remark, no doubt, from someone who doesn't have three older sisters." She grasped the shoulder strap of the cooler. "Let me help carry something."

He chuckled. "I'm sure you're right." He held out his arm so she could slip the long nylon handle from his shoulder. "Being the youngest Sutton most likely gives you a unique perspective of family." He reached out to help her set the strap on her shoulder. When he did, his hand brushed against the neckline of her tee shirt, and, for a moment, he kept his fingertips resting on the bare skin just below her ear.

Waves of feelings rushed through her as she swallowed. Heat from his touch pulsed along her neck and made her cheeks burn. A slight sea breeze blew strands of her hair across her face, but she pushed them away as her gaze locked with his.

Gareth moved toward her and bent his head. Out of the corner of an eye, she saw sea oats swaying on the nearby sand dune, but her attention focused on the intensity of the deep blue eyes looking at her.

For an instant, Delaney forgot the beach, and the ocean, and the seagulls, and the Sutton sisters on the balcony just a few hundred feet from the boardwalk. All she saw and all that mattered was the look of need in his eyes, a need that reflected her own desire for him to kiss her.

Would he? Right there on the boardwalk in full view of her family's beach house, would Gareth Collins kiss her? She knew it was what she wanted, to feel his lips on hers. The consequences did not seem to matter then. She couldn't even think of any; but, of course, there would be consequences.

"Delaney." The low sound of his voice filled her ears with tingling anticipation. Her heart skipped a beat but did not have time to resume a normal rhythm before his mouth touched hers.

He moved his lips along hers in a slow, gentle motion that sent tiny shivers up and down her spine. She tried to inhale; but, with the huge expanse of air all around her, she couldn't seem to fill her lungs. The touch of his mouth took away every bit of her breath and left her with an awareness of warmth and acceptance she had never experienced before then.

The feeling was exhilarating and unnerving all at the same time. Emotions ebbed and flowed inside of her like the waves on the sand at the beach.

She tasted salt and sand and fresh air as his mouth pressed to hers and left her with a longing so power-ful that she wasn't sure she could continue to stand.

Grasping the railing along the boardwalk, she steadied herself against the onslaught of emotions that enveloped her.

"Oh, Delaney." His hoarse voice drifted to her ears as if they were attempting to penetrate a thick ocean fog. She felt him lift his head and then rest his chin on the top of her head. Shifting the pile of towels draped over on arm, he sighed. "I think your sisters saw that."

She nodded and took a step back from him. "Yes, I'm sure they did."

"I'm sorry."

"No, don't be."

"We'd better get up there to the balcony."

"Yes, probably."

She walked in silence beside him as she tried to make sense of what had just happened. Her mouth still tingled from the touch of his lips.

He sighed as his steps seemed to slow down when they neared her family's beach house. "I'm not sure I'll be able to offer a plausible explanation."

"A what?"

"An explanation. For my behavior. I usually don't do something so impulsive. I don't know—" He shook his head. "It's been on my mind—kissing you, I mean. In fact, you've been on my mind a lot. I can't seem to think of anything or anyone else."

So have you . . . been on my mind, I mean. Delaney felt the air rush from her lungs again, and she had a hard time drawing a breath. She swallowed. "They won't say anything in front of your nieces. I'm fairly sure they'll say nothing until you're gone."

"Who?"

"My sisters. They may be nosy and meddling, but Allison will make sure that Brianna and Cassie use proper manners. That's always been her job as the oldest, to make sure that we're polite in social situations."

"Oh, I see." He continued to walk in silence for a long moment. "I owe you an explanation too."

She shook her head as she stepped off the boardwalk onto the sand and crushed-shell path that led to the row of beach houses on each side of them. "No. It was an impulsive action, like you said. Let's just say our behavior was the result of an idyllic afternoon at the beach."

He smiled. "It was wonderful, Delaney."

"Yes, it was. Thank you."

"Are you sure about not explaining to your sisters?"

She nodded. "It's better this way."

"It's better for me, but probably not for you."

She smiled up at him. "Take the girls home. Have a relaxing evening."

"Are you really going to dress up like Squanto and perform a Native American dance?"

"I am unless I can figure out a way to avoid their persistent nagging." She sighed and glanced in the direction of her family's beach house. "They're all fairly persuasive."

He chuckled then, that low masculine laugh that brought a smile to her face and warmed her heart. He reached out and squeezed her shoulder. "Somehow I have a feeling that Delaney Sutton is not the absolute victim that she claims to be. As a matter of fact, I have a feeling that she gets back at her sisters in subtle ways they don't even realize."

For a moment, she gazed into his searching blue eyes, and then she smiled. "You're probably right, but it's always been easier for me to let them think they're in control. They like that power."

With a grin, he nodded and dropped his hand. "It's my guess that you like it too."

She lifted the cooler from her shoulder and slipped it on his. "It'll be our secret, right? I wouldn't want to spoil their fun."

His smile broadened. "Yeah, okay—it'll be our secret. I promise. Now, I'd better get Lucie and Lizzie home before Jessica calls the county sheriff."

"He kissed you."

"What kind of kiss was it?"

"I couldn't see very well. I need details, Del."

Delaney sighed as she glanced at her three sisters sitting around the wicker table. In the center was a large stainless steel pot full of steamed clams, a heaping plate of corn on the cob, bowls of chowder, and a platter of boiled lobster. She had hoped that they could at least start eating their Cape Cod meal before a major interrogation began. After Gareth picked up his nieces and said good-bye, she had hurried to her room to shower and change into clean clothes. For the next few hours, she had managed to avoid any questions from her sisters until they had gathered around the table after they'd talked her into an embarrassing dance performance where she wore moccasins, a suede skirt, and a tunic with beads and fringe.

"Come on, Del. We need to know what's going on."

"We have a stake in this relationship."

"Did he kiss you or not?"

Brianna nodded as she passed a bowl of thick, creamy chowder to each of them. "Oh, he kissed her all right. It was a light, chaste one with no demands, but definitely one with vast potential."

"Brianna!" Allison reached across the table for her bowl as she chided the second-oldest Sutton. "It was a private moment between Delaney and Gareth. Perhaps we shouldn't ask too many questions."

"What?"

"No questions?"

Delaney watched Cassie and Brianna stare at Allison in obvious disbelief. Was her oldest sister actually taking her side for once?

"So, we're not going to talk about what happened between Del and Gareth on the beach?"

"We're not going to demand answers about that kiss he gave her?"

Allison smiled at Delaney. "Kissed her? I believe in reality it was Delaney who kissed him."

"I did not!" The defensive tone of her denial struck

her like a churning wave hitting the sand during a tropical storm. The words slipped out of her mouth before she had a chance to consider the consequences.

Gareth had initiated that kiss on the beach. He had leaned down and brushed his lips across hers. She had certainly enjoyed it, but had her response been more than necessary?

"Let's eat. I'm hungry." Delaney dipped a spoon into her chowder. "Everything smells delicious, Bri." The aromas of the feast covering the table caused Delaney's mouth to water, but, despite her words to the contrary, she did not feel like enjoying it. Nervousness filled her thoughts and made her stomach uneasy.

To her relief, her sisters dropped the issue of the kiss on the beach and turned to other subjects, including the arrival of the rest of the Sutton family over the next few days. Although she was comforted, for the moment, that she was not the topic of conversation, she realized that they hadn't dropped the matter forever. That kiss would come up again; Delaney just did not know exactly when it would be.

Delaney helped Brianna wash the dishes and clean up the kitchen while Allison and Cassie put away leftover food. After a large pot of lobster, dozens of cobs of corn, and bowls upon bowls of chowder, Delaney thought that she and her sisters would not need to eat again for another week.

"Who's ready for dessert?" Brianna smoothed an

apron over her stomach and turned to the group busy clearing off the table in the beach house kitchen. "There's old English plum pudding just like the Pilgrims probably made, and cranberry cake with cranberries from the bogs on Cape Cod all ready to eat with fresh-brewed coffee." Brianna smiled. "Well, decaf for me, of course— and the cranberries aren't exactly from Cape Cod. They're from the store here on Hatteras Island, but they were grown on Cape Cod. I hope you saved room for the best part of our clambake celebration."

Delaney shook her head. If she continued to eat such enormous meals, she'd have to start exercising, or she'd be in no shape to return to work. She wondered if she could even climb a ladder after indulging in so much tender lobster, buttery cobs of corn, and creamy chowder.

"There's the doorbell." Cassie wiped her hands on a small towel. "I wonder who that could be."

"I'll get it." Allison handed Brianna a stack of ceramic dessert plates. "You and Delaney can help Brianna serve dessert. The coffee's almost ready."

Less than a minute later, Allison returned to the kitchen. A broad smile covered her face as she directed her attention to Delaney. "It's for you. A handsome admirer."

Handsome admirer? Delaney felt her cheeks burn. *It must be Gareth.* What did he want? She set the pan she had just wiped on the nearby countertop and hurried from the kitchen as she felt three pairs of gray eyes on her back.

She ran down the stairs to the first floor of the beach house. In the pine-paneled foyer, she found Gareth looking at a Sutton family portrait painted in muted oil colors the year Allison graduated from high school.

He smiled as he turned toward her. "Nice picture. I take it you're the skinny one with the braids. Have you always been the little one of the bunch?"

"I was twelve, and my speed made up for my lack of mass. I could outrun all of my sisters back then."

He nodded, grinning. "And can you still?"

"Outrun them? I don't know." She patted her stuffed stomach. "These days we tend to eat more than exercise. I could definitely beat Brianna and probably Allison. I'm not sure about Cassie. She works out a lot." Smiling, she sighed. "Speaking of eating, we're just getting ready to have dessert. Would you like to join us?"

He shook his head. "I don't want to intrude, but I found your sweater in the cooler when we got home."

He held out the cotton cardigan. "I wasn't sure if you'd need it for tonight."

"Thank you." Her heart somersaulted when her fingertips brushed his as she reached for the sweater. "But you wouldn't have had to bother."

"It wasn't . . . a bother, I mean." He stuffed his hands into the front pockets of his jeans. "Well, I'd better be going."

Delaney's mind raced with conflicting thoughts. *Go before I start thinking about kissing you. No, wait. Stay and kiss me again.* She swallowed. "How's Lizzie's foot?"

The warm smile on his handsome, tanned face widened, and her heart jumped. She remembered the feelings of his lips brushing hers. Her own mouth began to tingle from the memory.

"She'll be fine. She's been limping around, getting sympathy from everyone—but I'm sure, by tomorrow morning, she'll be running around chasing seagulls without a thought of her sore foot."

"Maybe she needs more hugs."

He nodded. "Yes, hugs can be very comforting."

Delaney looked into his deep blue eyes. There always seemed to be more than he wanted or planned to say, but then he stopped just short of verbalizing them. She inhaled a long, steady breath to try to calm her racing heart. "I think that may be a simplistic theory."

"Pardon me?"

"I think you imagine the effects of hugging to be a cure for all ailments, but there are so many problems people have that can't be helped by such a simple gesture and a little discussion about improving one's situation."

He stood with his hands in his pockets as he studied her. "I disagree."

"So, you believe that's all it takes to solve the problems of the world? Just hugs and talking?"

"Hugs, and talking, and *listening*—good listening is an essential element in dealing with life's difficulties."

She wasn't sure what he meant. "Tell me about your kids, the ones Lizzie mentioned."

"When I'm not helping my father and brother with the family plumbing and heating business, I'm a counselor at a private school in Richmond."

"You're a counselor?"

"Well, actually, my degree is in child psychology with a specialty in adolescent behavior. I work with delinquent young people."

"They talk with you and tell you about their problems?"

"They don't always—never right away. Most of the kids have been abused or abandoned. All of them have been in trouble with the law. They've learned to distrust everyone, especially adults who appear to want to help them."

"So these kids, your kids, have made some poor life choices, and your job is to get them back on their way to leading happy, fulfilling lives?"

"Well, that's the goal. We don't always succeed, of course."

"But that's your job as a psychologist, to delve into people's minds?" Uneasiness filled Delaney's thoughts as she imagined Gareth analyzing her comments one by one. The possibility that he could guess her most secret thoughts unnerved her. She wished she didn't find talking with him so comforting.

" 'Delve' is a little strong. Mostly I listen."

Yes, you listen. That's the problem. You listen too well.

He sighed and smiled as he removed his hands from his pockets. "I'd better go so you can get back to your dessert. Cute outfit, by the way."

She looked down at her suede skirt and fringed tunic. She had kicked off the moccasins soon after the dance, and her legs were tanned and bare from her knees down to the tips of her toes.

For a moment, she stared at the door he had opened and then closed behind him. He was a psychologist. That was just great!

"Are you sure we need this?" Cassie poked her head out of the wide, unzipped door of the nylon, free-standing tent. "Can't we just sit on the sand around the campfire and roast hotdogs and marshmallows that way? Why do we need a tent?"

Brianna arched her back and looked up at the early evening sky. "It feels like rain is coming. Is there a tropical storm in the forecast?"

"If it does more than sprinkle, we're taking this western camp-out inside, aren't we, Allison? This tent won't protect us from the serious kind of weather that can come up the coast."

Delaney listened to her sisters as she set bricks she had carried from the ground-floor beach house patio and added them to the circle already in the sand in front of the tent. "I heard that the sky's supposed to clear up and be star-filled later on tonight."

Cassie crawled through the open door of the nylon shelter and began to tie back the flaps. "Well, those clouds look pretty dark to me. I'll bet we're in for a really big storm. If the wind picks up, this little tent is probably going to blow right across the island into Pamlico Sound."

Brianna stretched her arms above her head. "Maybe we should have a contingency plan, Allison—just in case. The sky *does* look ominous."

Delaney turned to her oldest sister. "I wish you'd decide soon, before I carry any more of these bricks from the patio."

Allison shaded her eyes and peered down the beach. "The weather report didn't mention a storm, but I suppose we don't want to get caught in a downpour."

"Let's set up on the patio." Cassie lifted the pop-up tent with both hands. "We can put this right inside the family room with the sliding doors open. Instead of a campfire, we can use Dad's little charcoal grill on the cement in front of the door."

"Sit inside the tent and roast marshmallows while we watch the storm, just like we used to do when we were little." Brianna clapped her hands. "That's a great idea!"

Allison shrugged. "I didn't think it was going to storm, but okay."

Delaney sighed and picked up some bricks to carry back to the patio. It was going to be a very long evening.

Large drops of rain began to fall from thick, dark clouds before Delaney had carried the last bricks back to the beach house. Her tee shirt and shorts were wet and clinging to her skin as she made her way around the small iron grill that Cassie had already filled with charcoal and was dousing with lighter fluid.

Allison moved to one side so Delaney could sit down near the unzipped door of the tent, and Brianna handed her a ceramic bowl of hot, chunky chili. Pushing strands of wet hair from her face, she scooped her spoon into the bean-and-vegetable dish and took a bite of the spicy mixture. She nodded her thanks.

"Oh, this is scrumptious, Cassie. I'm starving."

"It's too bad we couldn't be on the beach."

Allison handed her empty chili bowl to Cassie. "Just look at that rain."

"Do you think we'll have to stay in this tent the whole evening?" Brianna peered out of the doorway.

Delaney followed her gaze and watched the edges of the charcoal begin to turn gray as it heated. "At least we can still roast the hotdogs, and the wind direction is blowing the right way to keep us fairly dry."

Cassie sighed. "I'd rather be looking out at the ocean, though, instead of at the dunes. Tonight's our last sojourn for the year. It's too bad the weather isn't cooperating."

"Oh, let's stop complaining, girls." Allison passed a

basket of corn muffins wrapped in a red-and-white-checkered cloth. "We Sutton sisters make the best of any situation, and we always have fun, no matter what happens, right?"

"Right!" Cassie and Brianna chorused.

Delaney rose to a squatting position. "I'll have some more chili if there's any left."

"I made a whole pot full." Cassie took her bowl and reached farther inside the tent to spoon more hot chili with a ladle. "Try a muffin. It's a new recipe. And here are butter, jam, and honey to spread on them. Eat up, girls."

After bowls of hot, spicy chili, buttery corn muffins, and several hotdogs roasted on long forks over charcoal briquettes, Delaney lay back on the floor of the nylon tent covered with flattened sleeping bags. Rubbing her stomach in gentle, circular motions, she groaned. "I'm so full. I'll never have to eat again."

Brianna swirled honey onto one half of a muffin and licked the tips of her fingers. "Don't be silly. There's still dessert to come."

"Yes, Cassie," Allison said. "What tasty treat have you planned for the western camp-out finale?"

Delaney groaned once again. "Don't even try to tempt me, Cassie. I couldn't eat another bite even if you paid me a whole month's salary."

Cassie leaned over and grinned. "Not even if I told you it was your most favorite treat when you were little, the one you always begged for when we went camping in the Smokey Mountains? You *really* couldn't eat another bite—not even then?"

Delaney stared up at her sister's sparkling gray eyes. "You don't mean—?"

"What is it?"

"Tell us, Cassie."

Delaney rose into a seated position. "You don't have all of the ingredients. We're not making—?'

"What is it?" Brianna repeated. "Clue the rest of us in, will you?"

Allison threw her arms into the air. "Stop being so mysterious!"

Cassie smiled as she continued to look at Delaney. "We're having s'mores." She pulled a canvas bag from a back corner of the tent and began to empty it.

"I have graham crackers, chocolate bars, and marshmallows."

"Oh, yum." Brianna grabbed the plastic bag of marshmallows, and ripping it open, popped a puff of white confection into her mouth.

"We're having s'mores?" Allison stared at the box of graham crackers. "I can't remember the last time I had these."

"I can't, either." Cassie pushed a marshmallow on each tong of a long-handled fork before giving it to Brianna. "That's why I thought we could roast marshmallows and melt chocolate to put between graham crackers, just like we used to do. It would be the perfect ending to our western camp-out sojourn."

She handed another fork with marshmallows to Allison. "Here, the coals are just right for roasting. Hold this over them until the marshmallows turn golden brown."

"I like mine with black along all the edges," Brianna said, as she held the white puffs almost on top of the glowing charcoal. "I like the taste of charred sugar with chocolate."

"Yuck—I don't!" Cassie leaned out of the tent door toward the small barbecue grill. "A pale tan color is how I like mine. When the marshmallows are crispy on the outside and gooey in the middle, it's like eating a little bit of heaven."

Allison laughed. "How about you, Delaney? Do you still prefer your marshmallows for this campfire delicacy the same way you did when you were little?"

"The same way exactly." Delaney took two white, sweet-smelling pieces from the bag and pushed them onto the fork her oldest sister had handed her. "I like to roast them until the outside just begins to expand and bubble out. I'm careful to take them from the heat before the outside shell starts to separate from the soft center."

Allison shook her head. "It's wonderful to know that some things never change."

Brianna blew a flame out at the end of her fork. "What do you mean?"

"We each still like our s'mores the identical way we

did when we were growing up. And we've managed to keep some childlike qualities even as adults."

Brianna patted her swollen abdomen. "But we've changed a lot too. I hope we've gotten more mature."

"We have, and we've gotten more responsible, too." Cassie nodded.

Delaney broke off a piece of chocolate bar and set it on a square of graham cracker. "And wiser—I think we're all wiser."

Cassie ate a roasted marshmallow from her fork. "I'm wondering if it was wise of you to let us watch you and Gareth on the boardwalk yesterday."

Delaney's shoulders slumped as she spread the gooey, sticky fluff on top of the chocolate with the tip of a finger. *Oh, no. Here it comes.*

Yes." Allison leaned toward the barbecue grill to roast more marshmallows. "That kiss you and Gareth shared was very interesting."

Brianna's head bobbed up and down as she licked marshmallow oozing out along the sides of two crackers squeezed together into a sandwich. "Dare we hope that he's *the one?*"

Delaney held her stack of crackers, chocolate, and marshmallows between the fingers of both hands and took a big, crunchy bite. Sweetness exploded inside her mouth and made her forget for a moment that her sisters were planning out her life for her.

Chapter Seven

Delaney took time to make another gooey marsh-mallow, chocolate, and graham cracker sandwich before responding to the Sutton sisters' observations that Gareth Collins was *the one* for her. She wiped cracker crumbs from her tee shirt and forced a smile. "Actually, I'm beginning to have second thoughts about him."

Cassie reached into the plastic bag for another marsh-mallow. "You're having second thoughts? What could you possibly be second-guessing?"

"I'm just really thinking about Gareth Collins and me, together, in a relationship."

"What kind of second thoughts are they, exactly?" Brianna broke off a piece of chocolate bar and took a bite.

Allison patted her arm. "What do you mean, Delaney?"

"Doesn't he kiss well?" Cassie leaned toward her. "Those lips of his look just perfect for kissing. What's wrong with him?"

"Nothing's wrong." Delaney allowed her mind to float back to the moment when his mouth touched hers, and they kissed as the ocean waves pulsed against the sand. *No—there is nothing wrong with Gareth's lips.* She swallowed. "The way he kisses is not the problem."

Brianna grinned and nudged Cassie with her elbow. "See, I told you she enjoyed that kiss on the beach. It was so obvious."

"How could you tell? You said you couldn't see them from the balcony."

Brianna nodded as she finished the candy bar. "I didn't have to *see* to tell. I know these things."

"You don't know anymore than the rest of us."

"I do, too. I could tell right away that Delaney liked that kiss."

"Girls, stop bickering." Allison turned to Delaney. "I think our little sister was going to explain what she meant about her 'second thoughts' comment. Let's let her continue."

Delaney looked around at the three sets of gray eyes waiting for her to speak again. She heaved a sigh. "I just don't think Gareth and I are right for each other."

"What do you mean, 'not right'?" Cassie stared at her. "He's the best match we've ever found for you."

Delaney shook her head. "No, I'm almost certain he's not for me."

Brianna grabbed her arm. "How can you be so sure?"

"He's handsome, he's charming, and he kisses well." Cassie shrugged. "What else matters?"

Delaney sighed again. "He's a good listener."

"There!" Brianna smiled. "That's another wonderful quality. So, what's the problem?"

"That is."

"What is?"

"Listening—his being a good listener is the problem."

Allison lifted her eyebrows. "It is?"

"Yes, he listens *too* well."

Cassie leaned toward her. "What's that supposed to mean?"

"He told me what his real job is—his profession."

Brianna slapped her arm. "He's not a podiatrist, is he? There's something about a doctor who spends all day examining people's feet that bothers me. I know the world needs podiatrists, but I hope Gareth isn't one. Or a spy—he doesn't work for the CIA, does he? We'd be worried all the time when he was away on some secret mission."

"Calm down, Bri, and let her talk."

Cassie handed Brianna the bag of marshmallows. "Here—eat."

Delaney shook her head. "No, Gareth is not a doctor or a secret agent. He's a child psychologist."

"He's a psychologist?"

"Wow!"

"Really?"

"That's interesting."

Cassie and Brianna volleyed comments back and forth until Allison waved a hand to silence them. "And you're uncomfortable with that, Delaney?"

"It's a little unnerving. Gareth works with delinquent teenagers. He counsels them."

Brianna pulled a marshmallow from the nearly empty bag. "What's so bad about that?"

"He listens to every word I say. He's so attentive and intuitive. He seems to know what I'm going to say before I say it."

Brianna chewed a bite of marshmallow and swallowed. "That could be a good thing—his reading your thoughts, I mean."

Cassie nodded. "Men, in general, do not necessarily have good instincts when it comes to someone else's feelings. To be married to one who actually picks up on your thoughts and emotions without your having to explain in detail may be in your favor, Del."

Allison slipped an arm around Delaney's shoulders. "But you're not convinced this quality in Gareth is a benefit, are you?"

"Well, why not?" Brianna popped the rest of the marshmallow into her mouth.

"I don't see what the big deal is, Del. So what if he listens to you and understands you? Isn't that the point of having a significant other in your life?"

Delaney smiled. "I have all of you. I share my thoughts

and feelings with you. Why do I need a man to complicate matters?"

Cassie rolled her eyes. "You may be hopeless."

Brianna leaned toward her. "Are you telling us that
you're not even going to pursue a relationship with
Gareth? You're not even going to try?"

Delaney shrugged. "It's not that big of a deal to me. I
don't need a serious relationship right now." *Do I? Is it a
big deal if I stop seeing Gareth because he listens to me?*
She touched her fingertips to her lips as she remembered
once again the kiss they had shared on the beach. *I guess
it might be a big deal. He kisses really well.*

"What are you afraid of, Delaney?"

Allison's quiet question pulled her back to the tent,
and camp-out, and roasting marshmallows. *Afraid—I'm
not afraid, am I?*

"She's scared Gareth will find out what she does for
a living." Cassie crunched a graham cracker. "I need
some milk. I can't eat graham crackers without milk.
Do we have any left?"

Brianna nodded. "There's a fresh half-gallon in the
refrigerator. So it's all about her career?"

Cassie nodded. "Isn't that right, Del? You're still
worried he'll find out and try to persuade you to pursue
another less-dangerous profession."

Delaney considered the question. Was that the problem, or was she afraid of something else? She liked
Gareth Collins. She liked him a lot. Sooner or later, he

was bound to find out she was a firefighter. She doubted that her feelings for him would change just because he knew what she did for a living.

Brianna pushed another marshmallow onto the tong of a long-handled fork. "But he should understand. He's a member of the volunteer fire department right here in the village. I'm sure he'd be supportive if he knew."

Delaney shook her head. "I've met few men who were actually thrilled that a woman they cared about entered burning buildings on a regular basis."

Cassie sighed. "Well, if you're not positively serious about seeing Gareth anymore, then I guess we'll just have to move on to Plan B." She fumbled around on the floor of the tent and then waved a folded newspaper in the air.

What now? Delaney's stomach turned. "Please don't tell me that's Plan B."

"There's an article in here about the Avon Community Days three weekends from now. It's sponsored by the volunteer fire department to raise money for some new equipment."

Allison glanced at the article. "Plan B is to attend the events of the Avon Community Days?"

Cassie nodded. "That's Delaney's last weekend here before she goes back to work."

That's if I go back to work. Delaney felt her stomach churn. She hadn't yet told her sisters about Chief Adler's recommendations to her before she left. She hadn't confided in them about her concerns that she might have chosen the wrong profession.

Brianna reached for the newspaper and began to scan the article. "What do the Avon Community Days have to do with Delaney?"

Cassie's gray eyes glistened. "There's an interesting fund-raising event on Friday night. I think I'll sign Del up for it if she hasn't made up her mind about Gareth by then."

An interesting event? Delaney groaned. "What kind of event?"

"It's a speed-dating event. Participants pay an entry fee, talk with the others for a set period of time, and then rank their first choice, second choice, and so on. At the end, a committee makes the final decision about pairing up the guys and girls for a night out on the following Saturday."

Brianna handed the newspaper back to Cassie. "Who pays for the dates?"

"Local businesses are donating flowers, limousine service, and dinners for two."

Brianna rubbed her palms together. "Oh, it sounds like fun."

"No, it doesn't."

"Oh, Del, it'll be perfect for you. Where else would you be able to meet and talk with twenty-five eligible men in one evening?"

Allison touched Cassie's arm. "How do you know they're eligible?"

"It's one of the rules. The article says only singles between twenty-one and forty can enter."

"No—I won't do it."

Cassie turned wide eyes to Delaney. "This is the best opportunity for you, Del. If you're serious about not wanting to pursue a relationship with Gareth, and I'd like to take time right now to voice my objection and to tell you that I think you're making the biggest mistake of your life, then you need to participate in this speed-dating event."

"Oh, come on, Delaney." Brianna grasped her arm. "You'll have a good time. All you have to do is talk for sixty seconds each with twenty-five different guys. What a great fund-raising idea!"

She turned to Allison. "Wouldn't that be a good way for one of your clubs to raise money? It's kind of a twist on the auction idea—you know, when men or women present themselves to be auctioned off for the evening and then plan a date with the person who bids the highest."

Delaney groaned again. An auction—that would probably be her sisters' next great concept in their persistent attempt to marry her off before the year ended.

Cassie nodded and tapped the newspaper with the back of her hand. "This is our solution. We'll find you the right man yet, Del!"

"Oh, this is such a sad night, Del. Come over and sit with me for a while. It's our last chance to stay up and talk together in this bedroom before everyone gets here tomorrow. I'll be moving all of my stuff into the bedroom down the hall to be with Tim." Cassie's gray eyes glistened with tears as she held her arms toward Delaney. "Sometimes I wish we never had to grow up. Wouldn't it be nice if things could stay exactly the same as they used to be?"

Delaney smiled and gave Cassie a quick hug before she scooped the sleeping Max into her arms and sat down cross-legged on the foot of her sister's twin bed. "If we never grew up, then you and Allison and Bri wouldn't be able to torment me about getting married and settling down."

Cassie's head bobbed up and down as tears spilled from her eyes. "I suppose you're right. I do miss you, though, and I worry about you."

Delaney smoothed the fur on Max's sleek body. The cat glared at her for a few moments, yawned, and then snuggled down into the place where her legs crossed. She met Cassie's tearful eyes. "I think you should stop worrying about me. Your husband is coming tomorrow, and he's planning on spending a nice vacation with you here on Hatteras Island. You should give your full attention to him, not to my social life or lack thereof."

"Oh, but Del, we've got to figure this out for you." She wiped her eyes with the backs of her hands. "Are you extremely sure you don't like Gareth?"

Delaney shook her head. "I *do* like him. I like him very much."

Cassie's shoulders slumped. "You like him, but he listens too well? I just don't understand you, Del." She shook her head. "I really think he likes you too."

"We hardly know each other."

Her sister's gray eyes sparkled. "But you're kindred spirits. You were meant to be together. I just know it."

Delaney glanced down at the dozing cat in her lap. "That's your romantic heart talking. You've always been such an idealist, believing in fairy tales and true love."

Cassie laughed. "Oh, and you haven't? I remember a time when all you talked about was falling in love, and getting married, and having children."

"I was very young and naïve."

"And you were idealistic. Del, the people of this world need as much idealism as they can get. Don't be afraid. Go in the direction your dreams are taking you."

My dreams? For a moment, she considered Cassie's last comment. It had been a long time since she had made decisions based on her dreams. *What do I want? Where is my life going?*

She smoothed the soft fur along Max's back and sighed. Her career had always been something that was definite. Was she sure of anything anymore? Was firefighting what she really wanted to do? How did Gareth Collins fit in with her decision about remaining in or leaving the fire department?

She lifted Max from her lap and set him next to her on the thick cotton comforter. After patting the cat between his ears, she uncrossed her legs and swung them over the edge of the bed. "I'm going to take a shower and go to bed."

"But I want to stay up and talk, Del." Cassie threw a pillow across the room at her and hit her in the back.

"Come on, Cassie. I'm tired."

"Be careful in there. I noticed that the drain in the tub wasn't working very well this morning." She tossed another pillow. "We may have to call our favorite plumber to take a look at it. You know? The one you're not sure you want to date?"

Delaney shook her head and lobbed a pillow back at her sister. "Don't you dare! I'll fix it myself before I'll let you call him." She shook her head. "Anyway, Dad and the guys will be here tomorrow. One of them should be able to do a simple drain repair."

Delaney ducked as Cassie tossed back the pillow. "You're just no fun. Absolutely none. Where has your sense of romance and adventure gone?"

Sighing, Delaney closed the bathroom door and turned on the shower. The water spraying on her arm and hand, as she adjusted the temperature, soothed her jumpy nerves.

Ever since she'd arrived on Hatteras Island, the days had rushed past her. She had taken no time to consider the one issue that she had to resolve while she was on vacation. She had not done any long, profound thinking about whether or not she was returning to her job with the Richmond Fire Department.

Not only had she not made a decision regarding her

career, but she also had to face the added complication of her meeting—and liking—Gareth Collins. It would have been one thing if he were simply a new, good friend; but he was more than that. She was attracted to him, and that scared her. She did not want to think about a serious relationship when she had to worry about the direction in which her future was heading.

With a heavy sigh, she stepped into the hot spray of the shower. She wished she could rid her mind of the overwhelming concerns bothering her as easily as the water washed away the sand and salty air and sunscreen of the day.

"Come on. Get up, Del!"

Delaney felt something soft strike the back of her head. She tried to pretend she was asleep, but another soft object hit her again.

"I know you're awake, you faker." The speaker bounced on the foot of Delaney's bed. "You've been tossing and turning all night, and calling out, and mumbling." Cassie leaned over her and scooped Max from Delaney's arms. "It's a wonder you get any rest at all the way you move around and never settle down for the whole night."

Cassie jumped up and down, and Max meowed. "Is something bothering you, Del? It certainly seems like something is really upsetting you."

Delaney covered her head with a pillow. "My sister—

she's the one who's upsetting me. As if you haven't noticed, I'm trying to sleep here."

Cassie yanked the pillow from her grasp. "Oh, you are not. Anyway, it's almost lunchtime."

Delaney opened one eye to glance at the alarm clock on the stand next to her bed. "Lunchtime? It's only ten-thirty."

"Yes, and that means it's time for a pillow fight!" Cassie tossed the pillow at her. "Bri and Allison are coming with their pillows too."

"Oh, no. Brianna uses feather ones."

"So?" Cassie hit her with another pillow.

Delaney tucked the comforter around her. "If one tears, there'll be feathers all over the place. Mom will have a fit when she gets here and sees the mess."

"Then we'll just vacuum. Oh, and, by the way, don't try to use the tub or shower in this bathroom. I had to take my shower in the bedroom next to this one. The drain really needs repairing."

Delaney heard the door open, and she peeked out from under the pillow to see Brianna's smiling face peering at her. She groaned. "Leave me alone!"

Brianna tossed a lumpy, well-worn pillow at the bed. "I heard it was time for a pillow fight."

"Me too." Allison poked her head above Brianna's. "And I made chocolate-chip cookies and peanut-butter brownies to eat afterward, just like we used to do when we were kids."

With a sigh, Delaney propped herself against the headboard. Irritated by her lack of willpower, she pushed strands of hair from her eyes. "Extra-chewy and ultra-thick ones?"

Allison nodded as she stepped into the bedroom. "They're just like you like them, Del."

Max meowed, stretched, and then jumped from Cassie's arms right onto Delaney's stomach. The feline glared at her and licked his left front paw.

Before she had a chance to remove Max, Brianna struck her arm with a lumpy pillow, and Allison tossed a soft, crochet-edged one onto the bed next to Delaney. She shook her head and threw one of her own pillows in the general direction of the door.

Cassie swatted her feet, and Brianna hit her with another feather pillow. Max hissed and leaped from the bed to the chair, and then to the lamp stand.

Smiling, Allison crossed the room to set a plate of cookies and brownies on the small table in front of the shaded windows and pushed back the curtains. "See, Del, it's daytime. You need to get up and stop sleeping away your life."

Cassie hit her with another pillow as Delaney put a hand over her eyes. "Stop! Stop! I think this could be classified as sibling abuse. I believe it's illegal to blind and maim the youngest sister of the family before noon."

"Maim?" Brianna laughed and brought a misshapen

pillow down on Delaney's stomach. "These feathers are light and airy. They could never hurt anyone."

"They're dried-up feathers of poor little geese that gave up their warmth for you, and those pillows are older than I am!"

Delaney wriggled as Cassie pulled the blankets off her and tugged at her baggy sweatshirt. She kicked as Allison threw a pillow at her legs.

"You look like you're dressed for winter, Del. Did you forget it's summer on Hatteras Island?"

Delaney grabbed at the blankets as Brianna struck her again. Just as she caught the corner of the comforter in her fingers, she heard the sound of fabric ripping. In an instant, feathers were flying in every direction. The stuffing of one of Brianna's pillows covered her hair, sweat suit, and bed. As a feather landed on her lips, she sputtered and jumped up on the mattress. "That's it! Now, you've done it!" She dropped the comforter and grasped a pillow with both hands.

"Girls!" With her sisters, Delaney turned to see her mother in the open doorway of the bedroom. As she pushed feathers and hair from her eyes, her gaze focused on the person standing behind Vivian Sutton.

Gareth Collins' blue eyes widened as he looked back at her. While she watched, the most charming smile she had ever seen formed on his lips, his wonderful, kissable lips. Delaney swallowed and brushed a feather from her cheek.

"That's the bathroom over there, isn't it, Mrs. Sutton?" His smile broadened. "I'll just take a look at that drain."

Gareth backed the Collins' Plumbing, Heating, and Air van out of the Sutton beach house driveway and glanced down at the clipboard on the seat beside him: Osprey Lane. His next job was a faulty air conditioner on Osprey Lane.

He shook his head and tried to focus his attention on the road ahead of him and the busy late morning traffic along the main highway that ran the length of Hatteras Island. Concentration on his job was going to be difficult, he realized, as he chuckled to himself.

The image of Delaney Sutton, in baggy sweatpants and sweatshirt on that bed with a pillow in her hand was enough to make anyone stop and stare, but that look of complete astonishment in those gorgeous gray eyes and her golden waves flying in every direction when she met his gaze was definitely a picture to amuse even the most depressed person. When she brushed a feather from her flushed cheek and fluttered her long, thick eyelashes, he thought his heart would melt.

She was the most incredible woman he had ever met, a contrast of mature femininity and childlike acceptance of her role as the youngest sister. She clearly enjoyed carefree celebration of time with her family, but also, just as clearly, battled a deep, solemn melancholy of some past event that she kept secret from him.

He knew he just had to figure out a way to learn more about her. Could he compete with that powerful relationship she shared with her sisters? He had never dated any woman who was so close to her siblings, but he couldn't get Delaney Sutton off his mind.

Gareth slowed the van and turned onto Osprey Lane. He had work to do. He had to repair an air-conditioning unit. His thoughts about Delaney would have to wait, but he knew he'd have a hard time dismissing from his mind the image of feathers flying around her blond waves and her big gray eyes staring at him from the bed, poised and ready to fling a pillow at one of her sisters.

Delaney leaned on the railing of the balcony outside the family room and looked toward the dunes as a balmy early evening breeze filled her lungs with the smells of the ocean. A lone seagull cawed and circled overhead, and sea oats danced above the sand.

"You seem far, far away, Delaney."

Allison's quiet words roused her from her focus on the sights and sounds of the sea. She forced a smile and wrapped her arms around her waist.

"The exact opposite, actually. I'm right here, in the moment, enjoying where I am."

"Because something in the place you came from makes you sad?"

Delaney snapped her head around to look at Allison, but her older sister appeared to be studying a small patch of grass waving in the breeze at the base of the dune in front of them. She tightened her arms and sighed. Allison knew something. Her oldest sister had always been the most perceptive of the Sutton women. Delaney cleared her throat. "What makes you say that?"

Allison turned and leaned against the railing next to Delaney. "Ever since you arrived here, you've been lost and preoccupied with your own thoughts. I've sensed that you've been reluctant to share them, not only with us, but with Gareth. That's why you're so quiet and pensive."

Delaney met Allison's gray eyes as her oldest sister waited in silent patience. From inside the family room, she could hear laughter and an occasional loud voice as the Sutton family spent their first day on vacation together.

"Hey, Mom, Uncle Will says he's not having a birth-day this year!"

Delaney watched her niece Susannah slide open the glass door and rush onto the balcony toward her mother. Her blond hair hung in braids on either side of her narrow freckled face, and her gray eyes sparkled.

"He says he thinks he'll skip his birthday this year. You can't skip a birthday, can you?" The seven-year-old grasped Allison's arm. "We're going to sing 'Happy Birthday' and help him unwrap presents. Who gets his gifts if he doesn't have a birthday?"

"Mom!" Stephanie Cabot followed her sister out onto the balcony. "Uncle Will says he doesn't think he wants to eat his birthday cake. Aunt Bri and I made his favorite, double chocolate layer cake with fluffy white frosting. He *has* to have a piece. And ice cream. We have *three* kinds of ice cream to go with it. Oh, Mom, this is just terrible!"

With a dramatic sigh, five-year-old Stephanie flung herself at her mother and wrapped her little arms around Allison's waist. Her large gray eyes were filled with tears.

Allison smoothed her younger daughter's hair and smiled down at her older daughter. "I think Uncle Will is just teasing, girls. You know how much he likes parties."

"Do you think he'll eat a piece of his cake?" Stephanie asked. "And some ice cream?"

"And will he open his presents? Remember the one we got him? We got him a jogging stroller so he can still go running even when the baby comes."

Allison nodded. "He'll open them. I've never known your Uncle Will to pass up a chance to get a present." Allison patted her daughters' shoulders. "I think you should tell him that if he doesn't celebrate, he won't get his gifts either—no party, no presents."

Stephanie wiped her wet cheeks with the backs of her hands. "And he won't get any cake or ice cream?"

Susannah nodded. "Come on, Steph. We'll go tell Uncle Will he'd better have his birthday this year."

"Hey, Del!" Cassie stepped onto the balcony as she dangled a set of keys from her fingers. "Come with me to the store to get fudge sauce. I can't eat ice cream without gobs of fudge sauce, and Bri forgot to get a jar when she picked up the other party snacks."

Allison smiled at Cassie as she set a hand on Delaney's arm. "I think our little sister needs some time to herself and probably doesn't want to go shopping right now. I'll go with you."

"Well, here you are, girls." Vivian Sutton opened the glass door and stepped out onto the balcony. "We wondered where you went. Come on in so we can have Will's birthday."

Cassie held up her keys. "We'll celebrate as soon as we get the fudge sauce, Mom."

Vivian smiled. "You know, it's too bad we didn't think to invite Delaney's young man to join us this evening."

Delaney groaned. "Mom, I'm twenty-six. I don't have a *young man*."

Vivian lifted brows above wide gray eyes. "Well, we should have invited your *boyfriend* then."

"Gareth is not my boyfriend."

Her mother smiled at her. "I saw how he looked at you earlier today, dear."

Cassie jabbed her elbow into Delaney's ribs. "See, even Mom can tell. Gareth likes you, Del. I think you should call and invite him to Will's party tonight."

Chapter Eight

Delaney sighed as she took one final look at the sea oats waving on the dunes before she headed back into the beach house to spend the evening with her family. She wished her sisters would stop trying to play matchmaker for her. Even her mother was attempting to force a relationship that didn't exist between her and Gareth Collins.

"Oh, Del, you're going to be so annoyed with me!" Cassie pulled open the sliding door and sprinted out to the railing from which Delaney had just turned. "You won't believe what happened at the store."

"They were out of fudge sauce?"

"No, no." Cassie shook her head as she held up a plastic bag. "I bought three jars, just in case."

"You bought three in case of what?"

"I bought three in case we run out. . . . Oh, listen. It

doesn't matter, Del. I really blew it. You're going to be so mad at me."

Delaney stared at her sister. "What are you talking about? I don't even like fudge sauce. I like fresh strawberries on French vanilla ice cream. Did you forget the strawberries?"

"No. I mean, yes." Cassie shook her head. "I mean, no, I didn't get them. Yes, I know you like them. Brianna already crushed up a whole bowl for you. Oh, Del, I told him."

"You told who? You told him what?"

"I saw Gareth at the store, and I told him."

"You told Gareth that I like fresh strawberries on my ice cream?"

Cassie grasped her arm. "We were just talking. I invited him to go to the beach with us on Sunday."

"You didn't? Oh, Cassie."

"I did, but that's not the problem."

What can be worse? Delaney's stomach turned with a nervous twist. "It's not?"

"No. It started when I invited him to Will's birthday party tonight, but he said he couldn't go because he had a volunteer firefighter meeting."

A sinking feeling enveloped her. "And then what happened?"

Cassie wrinkled her nose. "Then I accidentally mentioned that you were a professional firefighter in Richmond. I really goofed. I know you wanted to tell him, Del. I'm so sorry."

Delaney inhaled a long, deep breath of humid air. "It's okay. I should have told him before now."

"Are you sure you're not mad at me?"

"No, Cassie, I'm not mad." She forced a smile. "So Gareth already has other plans for Sunday too?"

Cassie shook her head as she squeezed Delaney's hand. "Oh, no, he's coming. He says he'll come by to go to the beach with us and then join us here for dinner afterward. He's bringing his nieces with him."

Delaney looked out over the sand dunes. Twilight had set in, and she could hardly see the silhouette of sea oats dancing on the dunes in the ocean breeze. Now he knew. Cassie had told Gareth about her work.

Now he knows what I do when I'm not on vacation. And he's coming to dinner. Delaney sighed. The situation with Gareth Collins was getting more and more complicated by the moment.

"Let's put another tower right here, Delaney." Gareth's niece, Lucie, pointed to one corner of the huge sand castle on the beach. "That way, the princess has a safe place to go if a dragon tries to attack her before the prince comes."

Allison's daughter, Stephanie, stared at the little girl. "Is there really a dragon?"

Lizzie shook her head. "No, but there could be."

Susannah smoothed the inside of the empty moat with the back of a plastic shovel. "We're just pretending, Steph. Go fill your pail with water so we can test this moat. We don't want it to leak."

Gareth whistled as he approached the group and stood a few feet from the elaborate sand structure. Water dripped from every part of him, and he shifted from one arm to the other the foam board he held in his hands. "Wow, you girls are doing a tremendous job!"

Lucie bobbed her head up and down. "We did it without you, Uncle Gareth. What took you such a long time out there in the water?"

Gareth brushed wet strands of hair from his forehead, and turned his gaze to Delaney who rose from the sand and wiped her hands on her tee shirt. He smiled at her. "I didn't expect to be so long. Cassie and Tim wanted to race." His words were breathless as his smile broadened. "Your sister's quick on a boogie board."

She nodded. "She's very competitive too. I'll bet she made you race with her until she won at least twice as many times as you."

Lizzie ran up to him and grasped his free hand. "Delaney helped us, Uncle Gareth. Did you know she was so good at building sand castles? She's almost as good as you."

He grinned as he tossed the foam board onto the sand and reached for a towel next to the nearby collapsible cooler. His blue eyes sparkled as he glanced at Delaney and then began to wipe his arms and legs. "I'm really sorry I took so long out there in the water. I planned to come back to help the girls."

Delaney shrugged. "I know how persuasive Cassie can be. The turrets were tricky, but we did okay."

"Hey, look at that thing. It's gigantic," Tim Maguire said as he headed up the beach holding Cassie's hand.

"That is some castle! Did you girls do this all by yourself?" Cassie kneeled in the sand next to the moat Stephanie and Lucie were filling with water from their plastic pails.

Lizzie nodded as her uncle pulled on a tee shirt. She smiled up at him. "Delaney helped us while Uncle Gareth was riding his boogie board."

"He does fairly well out there on the waves." Cassie smiled up at Gareth. "Tim and I'll watch the girls now. Why don't you and Delaney go have fun?"

Pushing wet hair from his forehead, Gareth turned to Delaney. "Will you join me for a walk up the beach?"

"Sure, but it can be just a short one." With her finger-tips, Cassie stirred the water in the moat. "Dad and Mom headed back to the beach house over a half hour ago to start the grill and get things ready. We'll be eating in a little while."

Gareth glanced at his waterproof wristwatch and nodded. "That's good, because I'm going to have to leave early to make some calls for the fire department." He turned to Cassie. "Are you sure you don't mind watching Lucie and Lizzie for a few minutes?"

Cassie grinned and waved her arm at him. "Go— Tim and I will keep a close eye on them."

Gareth looked at his nieces as they accompanied Allison's girls and Tim down to edge of the water with empty pails. Then he smiled and held out a hand to Delaney. "So, are you ready?"

Was she? For a moment she stared at his hand, outstretched and waiting for her response. Finally, she reached out and slipped her hand into his. An immediate sense of warmth and comfort washed over her as he gave her fingers a gentle squeeze and led the way toward damp sand where the waves rolled up and then retreated to the ocean again.

"Cassie promised a rousing game of charades after dinner tonight. I'm sorry I have to miss it."

Delaney fell into step next to him. She enjoyed the way his fingers laced with hers as he continued to hold her hand. "I'm surprised she didn't make you promise to come another night to play. Cassie doesn't usually give up so easily when she finds someone who likes to compete as much as she does."

"Don't you like competition?"

Her heart skipped a quick beat at the sound of his quiet, masculine voice. She was having a hard time concentrating on his questions when all she could think about was the way his rough fingers felt holding hers. She inhaled a deep, calming breath. "I've been competing since the day I was born. Being the youngest sister in the Sutton family dictates that I fight for my place, even if it's always at the bottom."

He chuckled. "Oh, I have a feeling you're not always on the bottom."

"No, not always—I guess I win my fair share of the

time, at least in contests based on physical skills. I can still run faster and farther than any of my sisters."

"Speaking of competition, I have a proposal for you. One of the guys from the department had to fly down to Tampa where his mother lives. I have to hurry home, to call around and find a replacement for him on our drill team."

Delaney hopped over a rushing wave approaching them from a diagonal direction. "What kind of drill team is it?"

He slowed his pace until she caught up to him again. "It's a five-man, or I should say a five-person, team to compete in events at the Community Days next weekend."

She nodded. "It's to raise money for your department, right?"

"Yes, and we need someone else for the team I'm on because Brad had to leave unexpectedly when his mother got sick." Gareth slipped his arm around her waist and guided her through a maze of seaweed that had collected in piles on the damp sand. "We already had to find someone to take Nate's place this year."

"You mean your brother? I didn't know he was a member of the department too."

He smiled down at her. "So's Jessica."

Jessica—your sister-in-law, Jessica, is also a volunteer firefighter? Delaney studied his profile as his arm slid from her back to her elbow and then down to clasp her hand again She couldn't help but wonder how he felt about a female member of his family being a volunteer firefighter and putting herself into dangerous situations whenever she went out on a call. She wished she could read his mind, just like he seemed to be able to do with hers.

"Yes, but she doesn't want to be on the drill team this year because she wants to join Nate and the girls as spectators. With Jess, and Nate, and Brad all unavailable, we're having a hard time filling the places on our team." He squeezed her hand. "That's where my proposal comes in. I was wondering if you'd be willing to compete in Brad's place with us. Otherwise, I'm going to have to really work the phones."

"Me—you're asking me to participate in your firefighter competition?" She tried to focus on Gareth's voice. Warmth from his touch reminded her that he was still holding her hand, still walking closely beside her, probably reading her thoughts and delving into her mind with his counseling aptitude. Did he know how much she was enjoying spending time with him?

"Well, yes, I thought you might enjoy it. Cassie told me that you're a firefighter in Richmond. I know you're on vacation, but I thought maybe . . ." His voice trailed off as he stopped and turned to look into her eyes. "It's just for fun—no high-level training competition like you're probably used to."

"Oh, I don't know, Gareth. Compete in front of a crowd?"

He smiled. "It's all for fun. The spectators are really

supportive, and it'll be interesting for us locals to see how we fare against a professional."

"I really don't think—"

He nodded. "It's fine, if you don't want to. Don't feel pressured into doing something you don't want to do." He smiled down at her. "Just give it some thought, okay?"

Before she had a chance to reply, he took her hand again and guided her around to face the direction from which they'd come. "We'd better be getting back. It must be almost time for dinner, and we probably shouldn't keep everyone waiting for us."

"Hurry, girls." Gareth stood in the doorway of the Sutton family room where Allison's daughters and his nieces were finishing their desserts of scoops of vanilla ice cream squeezed between two homemade peanut-butter-chocolate-chip cookies while they played a board game around the coffee table with Cassie and Delaney. "Gather up your things. We have to get going."

Delaney swallowed her last bite of cookie and ice cream and wiped her hands on a paper napkin as she lifted her eyes to Gareth's. As usual, she felt his gaze on her before she even turned in his direction. She'd been doing that all through dinner. Every time she glanced at him, he was studying her. *Why?*

"Oh, but we didn't finish the game, Uncle Gareth." Lizzie looked up as she sat ready to roll the dice in her palm.

"We're almost done." Cassie smiled up at him. "Can't you wait just a few more minutes?"

He lifted his brows above deep blue eyes. "I've already given you an extra half hour. We really need to go."

"What's your hurry?" Cassie patted the carpet next to Delaney as she moved to create a space between them big enough for Gareth to sit down on the floor too. "Come join us."

"We could start over, Uncle Gareth, if you want to play."

Delaney watched him shake his head as he stuffed his hands into the side pockets of his khaki shorts.

"No, don't start over. Just finish your game quickly."

After Lizzie played, Cassie rolled the dice and moved her piece along the spaces on the game board. "What's so important that you have to leave, anyway?"

Delaney handed the dice to Susannah and stared at the game board. She knew she needed to avoid Gareth's eyes, or her heart would start to flutter again, and she would have a hard time concentrating.

"I still have to make some calls and find someone to join my drill team on Saturday."

"Are you talking about your drill team for the fire department?"

"Yes, I need to find an individual willing to fill in for one of the guys who had to go out of town."

Cassie's gray eyes sparkled with interest. "You need someone to fill in doing what exactly?"

"We'll be competing over at the athletic field against

teams from our department and others around the area. We have a bucket race, a ladder climb, and a hose-connection-and-accuracy event in full turnout gear. The fastest team gets a prize, free hang-gliding rides at Jockey's Ridge in Nags Head. You should all come and watch. It's usually an entertaining day."

Cassie grinned. "I'll bet it is."

Gareth shifted his weight from one foot to the other. "It's all for fun, of course, and to raise money for the department."

Delaney watched Cassie nod. "And it's a very good cause. Can anyone join your team?"

"While I'd like to find someone who's familiar with the equipment we'll be using and someone who's not afraid to perform in front of a crowd, there are no specific requirements for the participants. There'll be a lot of people watching."

Cassie smiled. "I think I have just the person for you." She reached out and patted Delaney's arm. "I'm sure my sister the firefighter would be happy to help you out."

Delaney sighed. *Stay out of this, Cassie.* Her eyes darted to Gareth, who met her gaze with uplifted brows and a question in his handsome face.

"I don't think so. I'm afraid I've already asked her."

Cassie gave Delaney's arm a playful punch. "You were just saying last night that you're getting out of shape here on vacation. You eat, and sleep, and never get enough exercise. Here's your chance to work out a little, doing stuff you love to do."

Gareth's blue eyes held a silent appeal that Delaney tried to ignore. "I don't have my turnout gear with me."

"I'm sure the department has extra sets. Don't you, Gareth? Couldn't you find something for Del to use?"

He nodded. "Yes, of course, we could—but I've already mentioned the idea to Delaney, and I don't think she—"

Cassie curled her arm around Delaney's back and nudged her toward Gareth. "Tell him you'll join that drill team competition. It'll be the perfect activity for you to get some exercise and to help Gareth's department out, all at the same time."

Delaney dropped her shoulders. It was going to be a losing battle for her now that Cassie knew about the firefighting competition. Her sister was too persistent. She would not leave Delaney alone until she agreed to join Gareth Collins' team.

"All right. I'll do it, if you can't find anyone else." Delaney raised her gaze to the man standing in the doorway of the family room as Cassie clapped her hands. When Delaney shook her head, he smiled at her. *What have I done? What am I getting myself into now?*

"I'm not going."

"What do you mean, Del? You have to go."

"Cassie and I signed you up and paid your entry fee. You have to go."

"I think Delaney is just surprised." Allison slipped

her arm around Delaney's shoulders. "She just needs a few minutes to adjust to the idea."

Delaney shrugged off her oldest sister's arms and pulled Max into her lap. He snuggled against her stomach and purred. "I'm not ever going to adjust to the idea. I told you I didn't want to participate in that speed-dating event."

"Oh, come on, Del. It'll be fun."

Brianna's blond head bobbed up and down. "We'll all go and cheer you on. You may even meet a nice guy or two. There'll be twenty-five to choose from."

Delaney groaned. *That means twenty-five strangers with whom to have to make conversation.* She smoothed the soft fur over Max's back.

"Maybe Delaney doesn't want to meet anyone else because she's found the man who's perfect for her."

Delaney glared at Allison. "If you're referring to Gareth Collins, you're wrong. He's not perfect for me. We haven't even seen each other since Sunday when he went to the beach with us."

"And then he had dinner here." Brianna said. "Don't forget that."

Cassie grinned. "And he's called you—twice."

Delaney narrowed her eyes. "Yeah—first he called to let me know he found turnout gear to fit me, and next to tell me the time we have to meet at the athletic field tomorrow morning. Thanks to you, I have to get up by eight to be ready to practice with the drill team. I think I hate you."

Cassie smiled. "You don't hate me. You know I'm looking out for your best interests. Come on. Let's find something gorgeous for you to wear tonight."

Brianna rubbed her back and rose from Cassie's bed. "I think you should wear your blue-and-yellow-print dress, the cotton one with the V-neck and shirred waist."

"Ooo, that's a good choice." Allison smiled. "Wear it with your yellow flats."

Cassie tugged on her arm. Come on, Del. You have only an hour to get ready and go over to the Driftwood Inn."

"I told you—I'm not going to the Driftwood Inn." Max yawned as Delaney crossed her arms.

Brianna nodded. "You just have to go. They're having half-price drinks and appetizers during the speed-dating event. From what I understand, all the participants will be at tables on the dance floor, and we spectators will watch from our seats all around it."

Delaney felt her eyes grow wide. "People are going to be *listening* to the conversations of the participants?"

Brianna's head bobbed up and down. "We'll listen as best we can. There are twenty-five tables, but we're going to get there early and find seats right near your table so we can hear you. It'll be so fun."

Cassie nodded. "The women stay in their seats while the men move from table to table. And get this: You don't have to choose your date for tomorrow night. The judges will be wandering around watching and listening, and they'll make the final choices of who goes out with whom."

Delaney's mood was sinking to a very low point. "They'll decide based on what?"

Cassie shrugged. "Well, they'll probably base the final decision on something ridiculous like matching sock color or other arbitrary things like that. Maybe they'll pair people up by their first names or their outfits."

Delaney scratched under Max's chin. "They'd determine compatability based on *outfits?*"

"The event is supposed to be fun and silly to raise money and provide entertainment. Don't be so serious about it."

Brianna gave her arm a gentle punch. "Yes, be a good sport and get dressed. If you do this and don't like your date tomorrow night, we promise not to bug you again for the rest of your vacation about finding a man."

Delaney looked from one set of gray eyes to the next and then settled her gaze on Allison. "Really—you promise?"

All of her sisters shared a glance with each other and then nodded and said in unison, "We promise."

Cassie jumped off the bed she'd used when Delaney first arrived at the beach house. "Now, hurry and get dressed. Where did you put that little bunch of crepe myrtle blossoms, Allison? I'll attach them to the brim of Delaney's hat with a piece of white satin ribbon I found in the closet in the family room."

"I'm not wearing a hat, Cassie." Delaney chewed her bottom lip for a moment and considered the idea of her sisters not mentioning marriage or dating for the remainder of her time on Hatteras Island. The thought sounded wonderful, but it was almost too good to be true.

"But you have to wear the hat and the gloves. It's part of your—" Brianna's voice faded as her cheeks blushed, and she covered her mouth with her hand.

Delaney narrowed her eyes. "It's part of my what?"

"Oh, it's nothing, Del."

She stared at Cassie. "No, there *is* something. What are you not telling me—Cassie, Brianna, Allison? Someone had better tell me what's going on."

"We honestly didn't know when we signed you up, Del."

"No, we had no idea."

Allison set her hand on Delaney's shoulder. "It really doesn't make any difference, actually."

Delaney shrugged off her sister's hand as Max gave her a look of annoyance and then yawned. "I wish someone would just tell me what this secret is that you're keeping from me."

"It's no secret," Brianna remarked with a sigh, "at least, not anymore."

"It has a costume theme, Del."

"What does?"

"The speed-dating event—the participants are all going in costume."

Delaney had known there was a catch. There was always a catch when the Sutton sisters made a promise that sounded too good to be true. She just had not realized how bad it could be. "Do you mean like Halloween costumes?"

Brianna bobbed her head. "Yes, except there won't be any masks."

Cassie shrugged. "It's just costumes—any kinds, all kinds. You're going as a garden party hostess."

It could be worse. Delaney chewed her bottom lip. *I could have to go as a Hawaiian hula dancer in a floral curtain or a clown with multi-colored hair and a big red nose.*

Brianna rubbed her hands together. "Oh, isn't this exciting? I wonder who the judges will match you with."

"I thought this was a *dating* event. Why don't we get to choose our own date for the evening?"

"In real speed-dating, not all of the participants are matched up. Maybe one or two couples get together, Del."

"But this one's a fund-raiser, and the people who paid the entry fee want to have a date. What about all of the dinners the sponsoring restaurants planned? If everyone is matched up in the end by the judges, then each of the participants gets a date."

Delaney scratched behind Max's left ear. "So participants could be matched with individuals they don't like?"

"It's only for one evening."

"You pick your favorite dates from one to twenty-five, and the judges do the same thing based on the costumes you're wearing, or whatever, and then they put all of the choices together and announce the pairs for dinner. I'll bet you'll find your true love at the Driftwood Inn tonight."

Delaney sighed. "And even if I don't, you promised to leave me alone about the crazy idea of my being engaged by Christmas—no more dates, no more bets, no more trying to run my social life, right?"

All three of her sisters exchanged glances with each other. Then they nodded. "We promise."

Allison patted her back. "Now, hurry. We're heading over to the Driftwood Inn in less than an hour."

Delaney adjusted the wide brim of her hat and shook her head as she caught the smiling looks of her three sisters and the rest of her family crowded around a corner table near the one to which she'd been assigned on the dance floor. She had already talked with a resort manager dressed up as Blackbeard the pirate, a restaurant owner donned in fishing attire, and numerous local residents dressed as surfers, scuba divers, sea captains, and even Croatans—members of one of the Native American tribes that once inhabited the Outer Banks.

She hadn't kept close track, but she calculated that she'd carried on minute-long conversations with each of at least twenty men. Glancing at her watch, she wondered which one she would designate as her first choice of companion for Saturday evening's dinner.

Maybe she should just leave the choice up to the

judges. She had to admit that, so far, the conversations had not been altogether unbearable, although she did tend to listen more than speak most of the time. She found that the majority of the male participants were eager to deliver their pre-rehearsed speeches and didn't require more from her than an occasional nod, smile, or one-word response.

"Delaney."

She snapped her head around to look at the man approaching her table. Holding her hat in place, she stared up into a pair of familiar, expressive blue eyes. *Gareth?*

He wore leather sandals, baggy cargo shorts, and a Hawaiian-print shirt that buttoned down the front. Around his neck hung a camera, and he held a folded map of the Outer Banks in one hand. "I didn't expect to see you here."

She shook her head to clear her mind and to make sure she wasn't imagining him as her heart began to race. She watched him slide into the chair across from her at the small table. "I'm a little surprised, myself." Her words came out in a croaking whisper that she barely recognized, and she cleared her throat. "It wasn't my idea."

"It was your sisters'?"

She rolled her eyes and glanced at the table at which the Sutton family sat before returning her attention to him. He nodded to Allison, Brianna, and Cassie as they waved to him and called out friendly greetings.

When he pulled his gaze back to her, he was laughing. "Jessica signed me up and didn't bother to tell me until this afternoon. I almost didn't come. Apparently, my brother's wife thinks I need to get out more and meet people." He looked down at his shirt. "She even picked out my outfit. I feel ridiculous."

Delaney tugged at the gloves on her hands. "Me too."

He studied her from across the table. "That's a nice hat."

"Stop teasing." She sighed. "This is not like any speed-dating event I've ever heard of."

One corner of his mouth curled up into a lopsided grin that warmed her heart. When it skipped a beat, her mouth went dry. "I guess we do things a little differently here on Hatteras Island."

The sound of a buzzer filled her ears then to indicate to the male participants that it was time to move to the table of the next female in line. She stared at his charming smile and watched him rise from his seat.

"It was nice to see you, Delaney."

She forced a smile as a tall, blond man in a white sailor uniform and hat sat down across from her. She tried to focus on the fact that he was a summer resident of the island, but all she could hear was Gareth Collins' quiet laugh echoing through her mind.

Chapter Nine

"Isn't it just wonderful, Delaney? You and Gareth will have a great time tonight. I just know it." Brianna's eyes sparkled in the early morning sunlight as she poured a glass of orange juice from a pitcher on the wicker table. "I knew he was perfect for you, and the officials making the final matches thought so too."

Delaney tucked her legs underneath herself and picked apart a piece of cinnamon-raisin toast. "Yes, isn't it quite a coincidence? I think the whole evening was rigged." She narrowed her eyes and studied each one of her sisters sitting around the table. "Which one of you bribed the judges?"

"Oh, now, dear, I don't think anyone in this family would do that." Her mother reached out to pat Delaney's arm. "Brianna is right. This is fate. It seems that

165

you and Gareth Collins were meant to go out together this evening."

Delaney rolled her eyes as she set her piece of toast on the plate. Her mother could never believe that any of her daughters was as conniving and sneaky as Delaney knew they were.

Allison passed a bowl of purple and green grapes to her. "Here, you're going to need to eat something if you expect to win that firefighter competition this afternoon."

Delaney shook her head and passed the bowl of fruit to Cassie. "It is not my intention to win anything today. I'm just filling in for a missing department member as a favor to Gareth."

"Oh, Del, you have to try to win. I'll bet they've put you on the team as a ringer, hoping to collect the grand prize." Cassie threw a grape at Delaney.

"Stop that nonsense." Vivian Sutton removed the big bowl of grapes from the table and shook her head. "It took us almost two hours to clean up all of the feathers from your last friendly little battle. I won't do a major clean-up like that again."

Allison reached over to touch her mother's arm. "We aren't going to make a mess this morning, Mom. We just want to prepare Delaney with an inspiring pep talk before she goes over to the athletic field to practice."

"I don't need a pep talk. I really don't want to do this." She pushed away her full glass of orange juice and wiped her hands on a paper napkin. "I wish I hadn't let Cassie talk me into competing today."

"We'll all be there to cheer you on."

"Just wait. It'll be fun, Del."

Allison smiled. "Don't forget to put on sunscreen."

Her mother rose and gave her a hug. "Have a good time with your young man, dear."

"Hey, that was great, team!"

Delaney removed the helmet she had borrowed and wiped her hand across her forehead as she listened to the leader of their five-person group deliver instructions for the final event of the firefighters' competition. Without intentionally meaning to do it, her gaze drifted to Gareth, who was standing beside her as he held his own helmet under his left arm.

A smear of dirt accented the side of his face, and perspiration beaded on his forehead and down his cheek. The early afternoon on Hatteras Island was hot and humid, with only an occasional breeze blowing to refresh the crowds of spectators and participants of the Community Days event.

Delaney struggled to shift her weight from one oversized boot to the other as she tried to focus on the leader's words. They had already filled an empty trough with buckets of water, and connected couplings on hoses to aim a stream of water to strike a target. The ladder climb was the last event.

She was sweating inside the heavy uniform. Her tee shirt felt damp against her skin underneath the thigh-length jacket she was wearing. Performing the activities in shorts and a tank top on such a hot day would have been much more enjoyable.

Wearing full turnout gear, while participating in the outdoor event, made her tired and uncomfortable. She was glad the competition was almost finished.

"Okay, everybody, we'll climb the ladder in this order. Jim, you're first. When you get to the top platform, hang your helmet on a hook and then head back down." He patted another member of the team on the back. "You'll be next. I'll be third in line, and Gareth, you can follow me." The team leader nodded to Delaney. "You're the smallest and quickest we have, so I want you to take up the last position in this ladder climb. Scramble up, and put your helmet on the remaining hook before getting back down and running to the finish line over by the concessions stand."

Another one of the team slapped her on the back. "We're counting on you, Sutton. We have a real chance of winning this thing with your help."

Somewhere nearby a blow horn sounded to announce the start of the last event. Gareth set his helmet on his head and adjusted the strap under his chin as he smiled at Delaney. "It's just for fun, remember. There's no pressure."

She adjusted her own helmet and walked with him toward the starting line. "It's just for fun—right."

He touched her shoulder with his hand. "No, I mean it. The guys and I really appreciate your helping us out today, but I reminded them that this was your vacation *away* from firefighting."

She lined up behind him as the blow horn sounded again. The first member of each competing team ran down the hard-packed dirt lanes marked with white chalk that ended at the bottom of twenty-foot-high ladders set against a wooden platform.

The early afternoon sun shone in her eyes as she attempted to watch the progression of the race. Perspiration ran down her back inside her heavy coat. Her face felt hot and flushed.

One after the other, the local firefighters ascended the ladders at the end of the running lane and then set their helmets on the hooks that were mounted on poles on the platform before they descended. Gareth waved to her as his turn approached.

She watched his long legs cover the distance, both on the ground and up the ladder. In no time at all, he seemed to be back tugging the sleeve of her coat to tell her it was her turn to go.

Trying not to think about how hot she was in the bulky turnout gear, Delaney headed toward the bottom rung of the ladder. The meager breeze had stopped blowing across the large field as she hurried along the dirt lane toward the scaffolding holding the horizontal platform. Shouts from the watching crowd hummed in her ears and made her head throb. She was sweaty and exhausted. Her boots felt heavy on her feet. Nausea filled her stomach as she reached the bottom of the ladder.

Despite the headache and sick feeling she was experiencing, she climbed with automatic movements toward the platform; but as she neared the top, her feet became heavier and heavier. She began to stumble. The noise of the crowd became distant and muffled.

Her head spun as she pulled a glove from her left hand and then fumbled to remove her helmet. From somewhere far away, someone called her name.

Twice, she tried to set the hat on the hook before she got the strap to remain in place, and then she turned to head back down the ladder. It was at that moment that she heard the sharp shot of a firecracker. The noise cut through the hot, humid air, and, in an instant, the sound brought back to her mind the memory of the explosion over a year ago. The noise from that explosion had deafened her, and the force had thrown her to the concrete floor of the warehouse and knocked her unconscious.

In her mind, she saw again the blinding light and felt the nauseating pain as her body flew through the air and then hit the cement floor with a sickening thud. A few feet away from her lay a fellow firefighter. Her friend and colleague, Hal Barker, had been struck unconscious by the same explosion. He now lay silent and unmoving. The damage had been worse for him. His injuries were too extensive. He had not survived.

"Delaney! Are you all right?"

She forced her mind back to the ladder-climbing

event. She forced herself to concentrate on what was happening. She forced herself to listen to Gareth's voice.

"What's wrong, Delaney?"

"Sutton, get back down that ladder now! We have a good chance to win."

Swallowing the bitterness in her throat, she grasped the ladder and began to descend. After stepping onto the top two rungs, she braced her thighs against each side of it, and giving herself a slight push, she slid down the rest of the way. Hitting the ground, she ran with all of the energy she had left toward the finish line at the end of the lane.

Her teammates caught her as she crossed the chalk line and lifted her into the air. Cheers rang out from the crowd as she realized that her team had won the competition.

She pulled a hand through her damp hair and swayed on unsteady legs as the men set her back down on the ground. She wiped sweat from her face as she stumbled.

When someone reached out to catch her from falling, she looked up into Gareth Collins' dark blue eyes. His expression was full of apparent concern as he helped her unhook the clasps of her fire jacket.

"Hey, thanks, Sutton."

"You do good work for a girl!"

"Will you join us at the barbecue later?"

All of the team members tried to talk at once as Delaney sank down onto the bench of a wooden picnic table and slid the bulky jacket from her shoulders. Her head was still spinning, and her stomach tumbled with nausea.

"Here—drink this." Gareth thrust a bottle of spring water into her trembling hand and took a seat beside her. She watched him swallow the contents of his own bottle as she sipped hers with caution and tried to determine if the cold liquid would cause more churning.

He wiped his mouth with the back of his hand. "I need a shower."

"I need a nap."

He studied her for a few moments as the groups of participants and their families crowded around the tables near the concessions area. Congratulatory remarks and words of support filled her ears as she realized that the members of the Sutton family would soon be making their way over to them.

"Are you okay, Delaney? What happened up there on that platform?"

She allowed the cool water to slip down her throat as she tried to concentrate on his question. What *had* happened? Why had she thought of the explosion and Hal Barker at exactly the moment when she was trying to climb down off the platform?

The firecracker—that was what had startled her and made her stop what she'd been doing. The loud pop must have reminded her of the blast in the warehouse. The noise must have triggered her memory.

She hadn't forgotten the horrible incident. Details of that awful day had not faded from her mind at all.

The department doctor had warned that it would take time to get to a point where she wasn't reliving the frightening moments every day. Since she'd arrived on Hatteras Island, memories of Hal's death had plagued only her nights. Were they now starting to bother her during the day too?

"Delaney?"

She dragged herself back from her uneasy thoughts as she felt Gareth's hand on her arm and heard his soothing, quiet voice. Gazing into his blue eyes, once again she considered telling him the truth.

She took another drink of water. "I'm just tired. I haven't been sleeping well, I guess."

"I wish you would tell me, Delaney. Tell me what's bothering you and let me help."

The sound of his quiet, comforting words almost urged her to reveal to him her private worries—almost. She stared into his eyes and wondered how much longer she would be able to resist his gentle persuasion to confide in him.

"Hey, Del, congratulations!"

"You did a great job, little sister."

With reluctance, Delaney pulled herself away from the mysterious grip of Gareth's gaze. She watched as the Sutton family hurried toward the picnic table.

"What a finish that was!" Brianna smiled and inhaled several deep breaths. "That dramatic hesitation up on the platform was a nice touch. We were all waiting on the edge of our seats for you to hang up your helmet and get back down the ladder. You're such a performer, Delaney."

"Hey, Gareth!" Cassie gave his shoulder a punch with her fist. "You all did such a great job! Your team deserved first prize."

He nodded as he brushed damp strands of hair back from his forehead. "We get to take our hang-gliding rides next month on Jockey's Ridge." He turned to Delaney. "I hope you can make it back down to Nags Head to join us."

Next month? Delaney loved the sound of his quiet voice, but a lot could happen to a relationship in four weeks. She wondered where she'd be then, and if Gareth would still be a part of her life.

"I hope you and Delaney aren't going to get too tired on your big date tonight." Brianna grinned. "Remember, we're heading to the beach by ten tomorrow."

"Are you talking about ten in the morning?" Delaney stared at her. "You've got to be kidding. I was planning on sleeping in until at least noon."

Gareth sent her a look of obvious sympathy before turning to Brianna. "I promise to have your sister home by a reasonable hour."

Delaney inhaled a long, deep breath. "I'm not so sure about this date idea. I think I'd rather just sit in front of the television watching a good movie and eating popcorn."

She watched an emotion she could not identify flash

across Gareth's handsome face. *Was it surprise, confusion, disappointment?*

He met her gaze with questioning eyes. "You really don't want to go?"

"We don't have to."

He reached out to grasp her hand. "Of course we don't have to, but I've been looking forward to having dinner with you." He brushed the pad of his thumb across her knuckles. "Our meal's all paid for, remember? We can rent a movie and make popcorn later, if you're serious about that. I promise I'll smell better after I take a shower."

Then he smiled. She studied his face and his gorgeous, vibrant, uplifting smile that warmed her heart and made her mind race with thoughts of spending a quiet, romantic evening with a wonderful man like Gareth Collins. She sighed. "All right, I guess we can go, but don't pick me up until seven. I meant what I said about needing a nap."

"He's here!" Brianna rushed into the family room, where Delaney was smoothing Max's fur over his back as he dozed with his head on her lap.

"Well, come on, Del." Cassie followed Brianna toward the sofa. "Mom just went to let him in."

Delaney chewed her lower lip. "I don't want to do this."

"Sure you do." Allison pulled her to her feet. "You'll have fun."

Max yawned and stretched his front legs before jumping into Delaney's arms. The feline purred against her chest.

"See, Max wants me to stay home too."

"Oh, you two spend far too much time together already." Cassie scratched the cat's chin. "He'll sleep on your bed the whole time you're gone."

"He's going to get fur all over you." Brianna wrinkled her nose as Max swished his tail at her.

Cassie took Delaney's free hand and led her out of the family room. Delaney walked with reluctance to the foyer where Gareth was talking with her mother and father.

"Bring your brother, and sister-in-law, and the kids too," Rob Sutton said. "And, of course, your parents are welcome also."

"Yes," Vivian added with a nod, "we're always interested in meeting the family members of our girls' young men."

Oh, Mom. Delaney inhaled a deep breath and hurried toward the little group near the front door of the beach house. She forced a smile. "I'm all set."

Gareth turned and fixed his gaze on hers. His gorgeous, expressive eyes smiled at her before his mouth did. When his lips curved into a warm greeting of welcome, her heart stopped for a moment and then doubled its rhythm. Max cuddled closely to her and rubbed his head against her neck.

"Delaney." He took a step away from her parents. "You look lovely."

Cassie pushed her elbow, and Brianna gave her back a gentle nudge toward him. Allison reached out and squeezed her shoulder.

"Our little sister cleans up well, doesn't she?" Brianna laughed.

"It's a new dress." Cassie fingered the fabric of the simple pale green linen sheath. "We dragged her all the way to Nags Head to buy it this afternoon."

Delaney wrinkled her nose. "Needless to say, I didn't get that nap I wanted."

"I'm sorry." A grin tugged at the corners of his mouth. "I'm sorry about your nap, I mean—not about the dress. It's a nice dress. . . . Oh, these are for you." He thrust a bouquet of cut flowers toward her, and she caught it in her free hand. As she inhaled the heady mixture of floral scents, Max munched on a sprig of baby's breath.

"What beautiful flowers!" Brianna pushed aside the tissue paper in which the bouquet was wrapped.

Gareth shrugged "I'm afraid I can't take credit for them. They're part of tonight's package."

"It's a gorgeous bouquet." Allison leaned over to smell the blooms. "It just so happens that lilies are Delaney's favorite flower."

Gareth's blue eyes sparkled as he met Delaney's, and he reached out to scratch Max between his ears. "The florist wanted to give me roses, but I had a feeling you'd like something a little less customary. You're not the most traditional woman I've ever met."

What does that mean? Delaney didn't bother to ask.

"I'll put them in a vase." Cassie took the tissue-wrapped bouquet from her. "You two had better get going."

Max's robust purring filled Delaney's ears as Gareth continued to rub the sensitive spot between his ears. Her pet's response showed obvious approval of her date. She sighed. Apparently everyone agreed that she should go out with this handsome Hatteras Island man.

Brianna lifted the cat into her arms. "We'll take good care of Max."

Allison smiled. "Enjoy yourselves."

Her mother kissed her cheek. "Have a good time with your nice young man."

Delaney blew out a puff of air as Gareth slipped an arm around her waist and urged her toward the front door. She hoped they could get out of the house before any other member of her family said another word.

The limousine hired for the evening headed north to the village of Rodanthe and a casual two-story restaurant overlooking Pamlico Sound. The hostess showed Delaney and Gareth to a quiet, secluded corner of the second-floor deck. The center of the table glowed with the flame of a single large candle surrounded by a ring of seashells and protected from the evening breeze by a clear glass chimney.

"So this is the Anchor Inn. It's a pretty place." She slid into the chair Gareth held out for her. "I've never eaten here."

"It's famous for its fresh local seafood." He took a seat opposite her and picked up the menu printed on thick parchment paper. "This is where Nate and Jessica had their wedding reception."

Delaney waited while their server poured glasses of ice water. "How long has your brother been married?" She then asked.

"It'll be ten years this coming October. He and Jessica met in college."

"He's your only sibling, right?"

"Yes, but Jess is like a sister to me, and Lucie and Lizzie, well, I really enjoy being able to spend so much time with them. I'm looking forward to having a child or two of my own someday."

"But right now you're a contented bachelor?"

He smiled, and her heart skipped a beat. She pulled her eyes from his to stare at the flickering candle flame.

"I have been, yes, but Jess would really like to change that status soon. She thinks I need to settle down."

"And what about you? Do you think it's time for you to settle down?"

She lifted her gaze to his and met his gaze as his eyes darkened. For a moment, he didn't speak. Her ears hummed with the quiet conversations of the patrons at nearby tables.

"Until a few weeks ago, I hadn't given the idea much thought at all." He reached across the space between them and took her hands in his.

Warmth from his touch surprised her, and she

swallowed. Already knowing the answer, she asked the question that was on the tip of her tongue. "What happened a few weeks ago?"

His brows lifted just a fraction of an inch above his expressive eyes as they locked with hers. "I met a multi-colored cat with an ornery disposition and an extreme possessiveness of his owner."

"And this particular cat made you change your mind about your bachelorhood, or about whether or not to get a cat?"

"Delaney." He gave the fingers of both of her hands a gentle squeeze. "I met you. I saw your big gray eyes staring at me through the crack in the doorway as I repaired the washer at your family's beach house, and I knew then that my life had changed forever."

The serious tone of his voice astonished her. The way his hands caressed hers made her tremble.

"I had been dating casually for years, and despite my sister-in-law's less than subtle attempts to set me up with female friends and acquaintances, I'd never considered marrying any one of the women I met—that is, until I met you."

She felt her cheeks burn. "You don't actually know me at all, Gareth."

"I know enough. I know that I want to get to know you better, Delaney Sutton."

Their server approached the table with a bottle of chilled sparkling grape juice, and Gareth released her hands. "Are you ready to order, or do you need a little more time to decide?"

She cleared her throat. "I haven't looked at the choices."

Gareth turned to the server. "Give us a few more minutes, please."

With a long, unsteady breath, she lifted the parchment menu and scanned the entrées listed. Her heart was racing, and she had a hard time focusing on the printed words. "Have you ever had the sea scallops?"

"Yes." He nodded as he continued to peruse his own menu. "They're wrapped in bacon and served in a creamy butter sauce—delicious."

"Mmm, that does sound good. I'm also looking at the baked flounder with crushed peanuts and fresh herbs."

He smiled at her. "I think I'll get the shrimp scampi."

Delaney finally selected a dish of coconut shrimp and wild rice pilaf. Although she was sure the food was exceptional, she barely tasted it. Despite numerous tries, she couldn't stop thinking about the quiet, handsome man sitting across from her.

Instead of smelling fried seafood and tropical fruit, with each breath she inhaled the subtle scent of his soap and aftershave that wafted around her in every direction. After several attempts to swallow while the lump in her throat grew, she set her fork on her plate and pushed it away from her.

With probing eyes, Gareth studied her as a brilliant sunset settled across the calm waters of Pamlico Sound.

Delaney would have enjoyed the picturesque setting if her stomach hadn't been twisting in nervous knots.

"Don't you like the shrimp? I'll ask our server to have the cook prepare something else for you."

"No, no—it's fine."

He wiped his mouth with his napkin and leaned toward her. "Are you okay, Delaney?"

No, I'm not okay. I can't eat. I can't sleep. I'm not sure about what I want to do with the rest of my life. My sisters are betting that I'll be engaged by Christmas; and, to top it all off, I think I'm falling in love with a man who does not know me. No, I'm not okay. I'm actually a wreck. While she carried on an internal monologue, she tried, without success, to avoid his dark, seeking gaze. With a sigh, she caught her bottom lip between her teeth.

"I think you probably needed that nap you wanted."

His words surprised her, and she shook her head. "I did, but I couldn't convince my sisters of that. The Sutton women are a fairly determined bunch."

"They insisted on going shopping instead?"

"They also insisted on forcing me into a salon for a hair styling and a manicure." She held out her hands for him to see. "That was my first and last, by the way. Do you have any idea how much a manicure costs?"

He rubbed the pads of his thumbs over her nails that were covered with a coat of clear polish. "I'm afraid I don't, but I suppose a woman deserves some expensive pampering now and then."

Delaney rolled her eyes as she tried to ignore the way his gentle touch made her heart flutter. "You sound just like my sisters."

"Uh-oh, not the Sutton sisters—would they be offended that I agreed with them on this particular point?"

"Are you kidding? They'd be thrilled." She thought about the bet the older three sisters had regarding her engagement. Agreement about a manicure was not a marriage proposal, but she knew her sisters well enough to realize that they would be encouraged by such approval from the man they had hand-picked to be her husband.

Delaney sighed. "My sisters like you, Gareth. Whatever you say or do is just fine with them. My parents like you too. Even Max, my former loyal companion, likes you. It seems everyone approves of you."

He took a drink from his water glass. "And you, Delaney—what do you think?"

She listened to his quiet voice. The sound of it made her mouth go dry. "According to Brianna, you're nearly perfect."

He chuckled. "I believe your sister is an idealist when it comes to relationships."

"Yes, she is, although she has a point, I guess. She sees the good in everyone."

"But there *is* something bothering you about me, isn't there?" He reached across the table to cover her folded hands with his. "Have I done something that up-sets you?"

"No, you've done nothing wrong—of course not." She shook her head.

Now was the time. She needed to tell him. He de-served to know why she was so uncomfortable to share her concerns with him. She inhaled a slow, deep breath as he caressed her hands with his fingers. She tried to choose her words with care as her heart raced. She could not allow her growing feelings for Gareth to pre-vent her from being honest with him.

He waited with a patience that at once surprised and intrigued her.

When she finally began to speak, warmth from his touch seemed to provide her with the courage she needed. "About eighteen months ago, a close friend of mine died in an explosion at a fire in an abandoned warehouse. I was with him, right next to him, when it happened. For a while, I didn't recall the details. Those few, awful minutes of my life got buried somewhere in my mind."

Gareth nodded as he continued to hold her hands. His silent waiting kept her focused, and she inhaled an-other slow breath before proceeding.

"But then the memory of it came back, and I was forced to remember that I lost a close and trusted col-league that day. We had just climbed to the top floor of the building when something exploded—a pressur-ized tank, or a gas line maybe. The fire investigators never found out for sure. Both of us were knocked unconscious—but I woke up, and Hal didn't." She squeezed her eyes shut for a moment as tears blurred her vision. They began to pool and then sting as they rolled down her cheeks.

Still Gareth waited. The gentle pressure of his hand over hers soothed her nerves and calmed her spirit. She had never been with anyone who exuded such quiet serenity.

Blinking away the wetness, she looked into his eyes that were dark with concern. Without hesitating this time, she continued. "Hal and I were the same age. We attended fire school together. He was a close friend, a wonderful one who laughed and joked and enjoyed life." She swallowed. "Sometimes when you laugh, you remind me of him."

Gareth gazed at her with eyes full of reassurance and interest. He rubbed his fingertips over her knuckles and smiled as he waited.

"I feel lost without him at the firehouse. I feel emptiness at work where he should be. I remember how closely I came to dying and constantly wonder about why he died instead of me." A lump began to form in her throat. "The counselor I had to see after the incident said it's normal to feel this way, so anxious and guilty, when you survive a terrible ordeal in which someone else dies."

"Yes, it's a natural reaction, Delaney, to blame yourself for surviving a situation when a companion doesn't.

You're bound to experience some tremendous feelings. Undoubtedly some of them will relate to guilt. You're here, and others aren't. You can't change what happened."

"Sometimes the memories of that day make me sick to my stomach. That night on the roof at the Driftwood Inn when I became dizzy, I was thinking about the explosion."

He nodded. "And on the ladder climb during the competition today—is that what happened up on the platform? You were remembering the fire again?"

"At first it was just at night that I thought about it, but lately I've been bothered when I'm awake too."

"Your memories of the explosion are probably being triggered by the act of climbing. Both times, you were several feet high when you became dizzy and distressed, right?"

She sighed. "That's probably it, but it makes me feel so incompetent. After all, firefighters are supposed to be able to climb. It's part of their job."

He smiled. "I think you're being too hard on yourself, Delaney. You have to give yourself time to heal."

"But I'm supposed to already be healed. The doctors and therapists fixed everything."

"They fixed the physical injuries, yes. I'm talking about the emotional ones. The guilt you have about surviving a traumatic event in which others didn't is quite possibly creating tension that manifests itself in symptoms such as insomnia and bouts of anxiety like the one you had today during the ladder climbing competition. It often takes much longer for the mind to get better than it does for the body to recover from physical wounds." He smiled at her as he gave her hands a final squeeze and then released his hold on them. "It'll take awhile, Delaney. You can't rush these things."

A sudden sense of loss swept over her when she realized that his gentle hands were no longer caressing hers. She looked into his caring eyes.

He glanced down at her unfinished dinner. "Are you sure you don't want to order something else?"

"No, really, I don't, thank you."

"Would you like some dessert?"

She shook her head. "No thanks—I couldn't eat another bite right now."

"You wouldn't consider joining me for one song inside on the dance floor before we leave to go home, would you?"

Delaney held her breath as she listened to his quiet voice. Was there a pleading note in his tone? Did she hear more than a simple question? Was she imagining something that wasn't there?

She wanted to say "no" right away. No, she did not want to stay. No, she did not want to dance and to feel his strong, comforting arms around her. She wanted to go home and crawl into bed. She wanted to snuggle with Max and forget about everything, especially Gareth Collins and his charming smile, quiet voice, and soothing touch.

His deep blue eyes captured her gaze, and her stomach somersaulted. If only she could make herself immune to his compelling gaze.

"Come dance with me." His words were soft, and urging, and almost mesmerizing. For one last second she considered the consequences of being close to this man of whom she had grown so fond in the weeks that she'd been on Hatteras Island. She could neither explain nor deny the overwhelming effect his presence was having on her.

Her nod felt imperceptible; but when the smile on his tanned face broadened, she knew he must have seen it. She watched him set his napkin next to his plate and rise from his seat. Her breath caught in her throat as he held out his hand to her, and she recognized the happiness that was evident on his face.

Gareth led her inside to the dance floor where a band was playing a slow country melody. Delaney barely heard the music as one of his hands settled in the middle of her back and his other arm encircled her.

He urged her into the rhythm of the song with smooth, fluid movements that appeared effortless for him. She entered into the dance as she became the other part of a graceful team, displaying feelings and motions in a place where only they existed. Other patrons joined them, but it seemed to Delaney that she and Gareth were all alone in the room.

In her low-heeled shoes, she barely reached his shoulders as she glided with him around the dance floor.

When she realized that she'd forgotten to breathe, she inhaled his fresh masculine scent, and that sent her mind spinning and her heart racing.

Willing her body to return to the reality of the situation, she forced herself to tip her head back until she met his eyes. "I'm a professional firefighter." Her words sounded low and shaky to her, and the devastating smile that formed on his lips almost unnerved her.

"Yes, in Richmond—I know you are."

She shook her head. "No, no—I mean, it's my career. Fighting fires is what I get paid to do."

"Yes, Delaney, you fight fires for a living. It's your job."

She sighed. "I don't think you understand."

Dark brows lifted above sparkling eyes as he continued to look down at her. "I understand that your work can be perilous at times. I'm aware of the fact that you've recently experienced a traumatic, life-threatening event that has left you anxious and uncertain about the future."

The future? Yes, that was what was bothering her—the future, questions of her job and her life. She had to make some decisions before she left Hatteras Island the following week. Did she want to remain a professional firefighter?

"You lost a close friend, Delaney. It makes sense that you're at least thinking about making a career change."

Was she seriously thinking about making a career change? Her mouth felt dry. Except in her mind, she had not heard those words since her chief had suggested that

she take a hard look at her career. Hearing Gareth ver-
balize the problem caused a million doubts to swim in
her head again.

Her heart felt heavy. She hadn't made her decision
yet. She had just a few more days before the end of her
vacation. She would have to decide soon.

She cleared her throat. "I'm starting to feel very
tired. I'd like to leave now."

With a heavy heart, Gareth flopped down on the sofa
in the small living room of his bungalow and reached
for the bowl of popcorn on the nearby end table. Picking up the remote control, he turned on the television
but paid little attention to the news broadcast as he
stared at the fluffy, buttered popped kernels in the plastic bowl on his lap. He had no desire to sample them.

He should not have been there all by himself on that
particular Saturday night. He should not be watching
television or eating popcorn all alone. He should have
been spending the evening with Delaney Sutton.

What had happened? Their dinner-for-two prize from
the speed-dating event had been going well. The restaurant had been charming. Their table had looked perfect.
Their meal had tasted delicious. Delaney had appeared
exquisite in her new dress from her shopping spree in
Nags Head. Her blond curls had framed her sweet face,
and her gray eyes sparkled with obvious delight at the
picturesque setting and the warmhearted welcome they

had received from both the hostess and the manager of the Anchor Inn.

To Gareth's joy, Delaney had trusted him enough to open up to him about her private worries. She had appeared comfortable enough with him to share her doubts about her job. Relief had washed over him as she'd explained what had been tormenting her ever since he had met her that first morning when he was repairing the Sutton family's washer across the hall from her room.

Hope had replaced his uncertainties for a brief time; but then, sitting alone in his beach cottage and staring at the television, he felt disillusionment settle in around him. He had looked forward to Delaney returning with him. He had planned to watch a romantic comedy with her while they munched on popcorn, and laughed, and maybe held hands.

On the dance floor at the Anchor Inn, she had felt so right in his arms. As he had led her in slow, smooth steps to the rhythm of the country melody, she had moved with him as though they had been practicing together forever.

Everything had seemed wonderful. Then something had gone very wrong. What had happened? Why had Delaney insisted on going home so soon? What had he said or done?

Chapter Ten

"Okay, Del, tell us all about last night."

"Don't leave out a thing."

"We want to hear every bit of what happened."

Delaney shaded her eyes from the bright late-morning sun with one hand while she held Max in her other arm. Sighing, she plopped into a chair next to the kitchen balcony table and set her sleeping feline on her lap. She was not in the mood to deal with the Sutton sisters' unquenchable curiosity and endless questions so soon after waking up.

"Come on, Del. Give it to us." Cassie sat cross-legged on her chair next to Delaney. She reached out and scratched Max between his ears, and a loud, rumbling purr accompanied the insistent verbal urgings of her sisters.

"Yes. We're waiting to hear about your date with Gareth."

"You came home awfully soon."

"And you went right to bed."

Allison offered her orange juice. "How was the Anchor Inn?"

Welcoming the seemingly neutral subject, Delaney smoothed a hand across Max's back and smiled as she looked around the table at her sisters. Three pairs of expectant gray eyes met hers. "It's a quiet, comfortable place with quite a variety of entrées. We should take Mom and Dad there before we start heading back home this summer."

Allison handed Delaney a mug of steaming coffee. "I heard that many people hold private parties there."

Taking the cup in one hand while continuing to smooth Max's fur with the other, Delaney nodded. "Gareth's brother and sister-in-law had their wedding reception in one of the separate dining rooms."

"How nice." Brianna clapped her hands. "You talked about weddings."

Delaney wrinkled her nose. "I talked about Nate and Jessica's—no one else's."

"But at least the subject came up."

Cassie nodded. "That's a start anyway."

Brianna scowled. "Did you guys have a fight?"

Allison handed her a bowl of fresh apricots. "Tell us what happened at dinner."

Delaney remembered her conversation with Gareth

at the restaurant as she thought about what she should tell her sisters and what she should keep to herself. His words drifted through her mind: *"I never considered marriage seriously until I met you."* Delaney pulled her focus back to the Sutton sisters who were firing questions at her without giving her a chance to respond. She really just wanted to go back to bed and forget all about the previous night and Gareth Collins' expressive eyes and heart-warming smile. There was only one problem. As soon as she closed her own eyes, she knew exactly what would happen. Those deep blue eyes would instantly come to her mind and make her thoughts turn to him once again.

"We both had shrimp—scampi and coconut."

In her chair across the table, Brianna leaned toward her. "You shared entrées. How sweet that is! Which did you like better?"

Delaney shook her head. "I wasn't very hungry."

Cassie touched her arm. "You're not getting sick, are you?"

Brianna shook her head. "I'll bet she was nervous about being out on a romantic date with Gareth."

"I wasn't nervous. I just didn't feel like eating."

Allison leaned toward her and slipped an arm around her shoulders. "There's something else going on, isn't there? Something has been bothering you for days now. Why don't you tell us about it?"

Delaney inhaled a long, deep breath. For one last moment, she considered keeping the secret from her sisters, the one she had dared to share with Gareth Collins at the Anchor Inn. Finally she breathed through a sudden wave of dread and hesitancy and looked around at the three Sutton sisters sitting at the breakfast table with her. "I have to decide if I'm going to quit my job."

"You're thinking of quitting because of Gareth?"

She shook her head. "No, this is something I was thinking about before I came here, an issue that came up before I met him."

Brianna leaned forward in her chair. "Are you moving back home?"

Cassie grabbed her arm. "Do you want to live closer to all of us again?"

"Oh, Delaney, that would be wonderful!"

Delaney shook her head once more as another onslaught of questions confused her thoughts. "No, you don't understand. I'm thinking about quitting my work, my profession. I'm not sure I want to be a firefighter anymore."

Brianna stared at her from across the table. "But you love fighting fires."

Cassie nodded. "It's always been your dream."

"You're really having doubts about your career?"

Delaney stroked Max's fur and sighed. Fighting back tears, she told her sisters about her sleeplessness and the disturbing nightmares that had continued to occur long after her physical recovery from the injuries she'd sustained in the explosion over a year before.

Allison gave her arm another squeeze. "Being with Gareth has intensified these uncertainties about your work?"

Delaney nodded. "I don't want to make a decision based on what I think he wants, especially when I'm not even sure about what kind of relationship we have."

"We'll figure out a way to fix this, Del."

"There is absolutely nothing for you to figure out. I'm the one who has to do that. This is my career, my future. I have to decide what I'm going to do with the rest of my life."

Brianna leaned across the table and held Delaney's gaze. "But we want to help you. We're your sisters."

Cassie squeezed her arm. "Yes, it's our job to help our little sister."

Allison patted her shoulder. "We'll do everything we can to make things better for you."

Delaney forced a smile. "But that's part of the problem. You always try to fix things. Listen, sometimes things can't be fixed. Some things just weren't meant to be solved with a quick hug or a quiet weekend at the beach with the best sisters in the whole wide world." She inhaled a long, steady breath. "It's not that I don't appreciate all that you do for me. I love you all so much. I never would have made it this far without your tremendous support and encouragement, but now it's time for me to figure things out on my own. I have to resolve this question of my future. I have to decide if firefighting is still the best career for me. I have to determine if Gareth

Collins is going to be a part of my life, whether or not I continue in the same direction I've been going."

"But we're your sisters."

"We can help you."

"We just want to see you happy."

"Yes, and you're wonderful, but I mean it." She heaved another sigh of exasperation. "Allison, Brianna, I need no more interfering this time. Cassie, I need to do this on my own. This is my life. I'm a big girl." She tried to curb her growing frustration because her sisters refused to assure her that they'd leave her alone. In fact, they were no longer even looking at her. Their attention seemed to be focused completely away from the balcony. They had turned their heads to look up the beach.

She watched Allison furrow her brow before looking back at Delaney. The expression on her oldest sister's face alerted her nerves to some unnamed danger.

"What is it?"

Allison pointed up the beach. "Does that look like smoke to you?"

Brianna shook her head. "I'm not sure."

Cassie leaned forward in her chair. "It certainly smells like smoke."

Delaney looked in the direction her sisters were staring. Her heart jumped as she saw the thin billow of gray smoke puffing from a first-floor window of the beach house two doors up from the Sutton place.

Delaney jumped to her feet. "Call the fire department."

Brianna squealed. "Where are you going?"

Allison frowned and shook her head. "You can't go over there."

Cassie grasped her arm. "Del, wait for help."

Delaney shook her sister's hand from her arm and set Max on Cassie's lap. She headed toward the nearest set of stairs leading to the ground. "I'm just going to check things out. One of you needs to call nine-one-one!" Ignoring her sisters' shouts to stop, she rushed across the sandy area between the line of beach houses and the dunes. She barely felt the sting of a cactus plant pricking her foot as the sharp thorn penetrated her skin through a hole in her rubber sandals. As she approached the small, modest structure elevated on thick wooden pylons, she saw more smoke flooding from an open window.

A young brunett in shorts and a tee shirt ran up to her as she wrung her hands and then grasped Delaney's arm. "Help us, please!"

Delaney's stomach twisted into a tight knot. "Is someone still inside?"

The woman's eyes were full of an emotion that looked to Delaney like pure terror. She inhaled a deep breath and coughed from the smoky air. "Ma'am, do you know if anyone else is inside the house?"

The woman nodded with quick, sharp movements and the same expression of fear in her eyes. "My husband—" She gulped a breath of air. "He's in there."

Delaney's eyes followed the direction in which the woman pointed. She tried to keep her thoughts clear and calm, but the panic exuding from the stranger seemed to close in on her.

She stared at the open door that had the woman's attention. She saw no one, but smoke poured out from a window on the floor above the support beams. The entrance appeared to be clear at the moment. From somewhere inside the house, an activated smoke detector pierced the air.

The woman's grip on her arm tightened. "It's my son. We can't find him. We thought he was playing out on the deck, but when we heard the smoke alarm go off, we ran out to get him. He wasn't there. My husband went back inside to look for him." Tears streamed down her pale cheeks. "He hasn't come out yet. Oh, please help me find them!"

Delaney swallowed the fear that began to surge around her. She nodded as she squeezed the woman's hand and removed it from her arm. "Stay here. The fire department is on its way."

The stranger's eyes stared at her. "I have to find them. I can't just leave my son and husband in there in the fire."

"I'll go. You wait here."

She hoped the woman would follow her instructions as she ran up the steps and into the house. The last thing she needed right then was a panicky mother hurrying back into a burning building without any protective gear or training.

She looked around what appeared to be a small living

room as the acrid smell of burning wood and synthetic materials rushed into her lungs. She tried to focus her eyes in the smoke-filled area.

To her surprise, a tall male figure emerged through the foggy interior. His face was streaked with soot, and he coughed several times.

Delaney reached for his arm. "You need to get out."

His eyes held the same look of terror that the woman outside had. "I can't find my son."

Delaney swallowed the fear rising in her throat. She had to keep her head clear. She knew she needed to stay focused. "Are you sure your son is still in here?" She had to shout above the sharp whine of the smoke detector.

The man nodded as he searched the room with frantic eyes. "He was outside playing, but just before the smoke alarm went off, I thought I heard him come back in. Help me find Jerry. He's only four."

She touched the man's shoulder. "He's probably scared. Where are the bedrooms?"

"They're on the second floor." He pointed toward an open staircase at one end of the room. "His is the last door on the left, but I already checked."

She steered him toward the door. "He's probably hiding and didn't hear you calling. I'll find your son for you." Approaching sirens wailed in her ears as he appeared to hesitate. "Go outside. Your wife needs you."

"But Jerry—"

"I'm a trained firefighter. I'll find your son."

For a frightening moment, she thought he would protest, but then he turned and hurried through the open door. Delaney swallowed another wave of fear as she watched the tall man leave the beach house.

She ran across the room and up the stairs where the air became thick and heavy. The pungent odor of smoldering wood and other building materials stung her nose and filled her lungs. She coughed, and tears streamed down her cheeks as her eyes burned and watered.

At the top of the stairs, her legs swayed. Her arms shook. Her stomach twisted with nausea. In an instant, the memory of the explosion came back to her. She remembered the force that knocked her to the floor, drifting into unconsciousness, and then waking up and realizing that Hal, her friend and colleague, had not survived.

She swallowed as she tried to clear her mind and focus on the present, on Jerry. The frightened, four-year-old boy could be trapped somewhere in the burning beach house. The little boy's parents were counting on her to rescue him. With a strength she didn't know she possessed, she fought the feeling that she was going to fall backwards down the stairs, and she resisted the urge to give up the search she had begun. She grasped the railing and forced herself to think about finding the missing child.

She could not faint. She had to keep moving. Jerry needed her. His parents were entrusting his safe return to her. She couldn't fail. She wouldn't let them down. She was a firefighter, and knew what she had to do.

Dropping to the floor, she began to crawl through air that was so thick she could no longer see. She soon lost her sense of position and bumped her head into a wall. *On the left,* she reminded herself, *at the end of the hall.* She used her left hand to guide her along the carpeted hallway. The first door she came to was closed. "Jerry! Where are you?"

She strained to hear a child's voice or movement. The scream of sirens came closer to the house. Hearing nothing, she moved on to the next door, and then to the last. Unlike the others, it stood ajar. Delaney blinked to try to clear her vision to see into the room. Through the gray, smoky haze, she could distinguish a twin bed against one wall, a basketball next to it, and some toy trucks and race cars strewn around on the floor. It was clearly a child's room.

She tried to call to the little boy, but no sound came out of her mouth. Clearing her throat, she tried again. "Jerry, are you here?"

She listened with careful attention, but all she heard was the piercing wail of approaching sirens. She moved farther into the bedroom.

"Jerry, my name is Delaney. I'm here to help you."

She coughed again as her lungs longed for fresh, clean air. Nausea twisted in her stomach, but she rose to her feet and moved across the carpeted floor. Spying a plastic container that looked like a toy chest, she lifted the lid. She peered inside it, but saw only toys. Then she leaned down to look under the bed. She choked on smoke as she stared into empty space.

"Jerry, please talk to me." She tried to keep her voice calm. She could not panic.

She thought she heard a shuffling noise. On the wall opposite the bed, there was a door that appeared to lead to a closet or a storage area of some kind.

"I'll keep you safe, Jerry."

She reached for the knob and held her breath as she pulled open the door. She thought she heard a whimper. Her eyes burned as she stared into the darkness. Tears caused by the smoke streamed down her face. "Your mom and dad are waiting for you."

The roar of large truck engines filled the air. She tried to focus her eyes on the enclosed space as she held out her hand. "They asked me to take you to them, Jerry."

She saw a box move, and then a little head appeared. Relief flooded over her as two large, glistening eyes stared up at her. She looked at the tear-stained face of the small boy clutching a ragged stuffed rabbit. "Hi, Jerry. I'm Delaney."

She heard loud footsteps thud in the distance and watched the child's eyes grow into huge balls. Tears spilled down his cheeks as he shrank back into the shadows.

"It's okay, Jerry. That's the firefighters. We need to leave so they can come in and find what's making all of this smoke."

With hesitant movements, the child scooted toward her as he clutched the worn cloth toy. She reached out to him and scooped the small child into her arms.

He trembled as she held him and then turned to head out of the room. "It's going to be okay, Jerry. You'll be with your mom and dad soon."

Cautiously, she stepped into the hall. Although it was filled with smoke, she could see no flames or feel any increase in temperature. If a fire was burning some-where in the house, it appeared to be contained away from the second floor and stairs.

Holding Jerry securely in her arms, she leaned for-ward and rushed through the corridor clouded with soot to the steps she had just climbed. At the top of the stair-case, she felt her legs begin to shake. Her head spun from lack of fresh air and the panic that threatened to take control of her movements.

The little boy shifted in her arms and reminded her once again of her reason for being there. His parents were waiting for him. They were counting on her to res-cue their son and deliver him safely to them. She could do that. She was almost there.

With renewed confidence, she pushed herself for-ward and began to descend the stairs. At the bottom, she blinked as smoke stung her eyes when she tried to recall the direction she needed to go to get to the door leading out to the side yard from which she'd first en-tered the house. The smoky air seemed to be less thick than it had been upstairs, but her eyes were tearing so much that she could barely focus on the details of the interior of the room.

Securing her arms around the child, she stumbled in the general direction of the nearest exit from the house. She kept her head down, her shoulders slouched, and her eyes closed while trying to breathe in as little of the sooty air as possible. Reaching the door, she rose again to her full height. With aching back and shoulder muscles from the strain of carrying the child, she adjusted her hold again and took another step. To her surprise, she smashed into something hard and immoveable.

Startled, she looked up into a pair of familiar blue eyes that were staring back at her through a clear protective firefighter shield: Gareth Collins. Her arms pressed against muscle and strength beneath a layer of fire-resistant fabric as he gazed at her from under the brim of his yellow fiberglass helmet. His face broke into a smile of recognition and concern. Another wave of relief flooded her senses.

Gareth lifted a gloved hand and patted Jerry's head. The little boy whimpered and clung to his stuffed rabbit.

She watched Gareth nod, and then felt him drape an arm around her shoulders. He guided her with the child through the doorway and onto the open porch.

Hot sunlight struck her face and arms as she stepped out into the fresh ocean air. She couldn't stop coughing as Gareth led her down the steps and across the sand-and-grass lawn.

She was aware of Jerry's parents rushing toward her

and taking the little boy from her. Her empty arms felt heavy and sore as she continued to cough and tried to fill her lungs with air.

It took great effort to catch her breath and to walk at the same time, and her legs seemed unable to hold her. When she attempted to regain her balance, Gareth put one arm around her waist and then lifted her until she was cradled in a comforting hold against his firm chest. With steady steps, he carried her across two lots to the nearby street. He set her on the diamond-plated tailgate of an open rescue squad vehicle.

A uniformed paramedic placed a mask over her nose and mouth while another one checked her pulse and blood pressure. As soon as she inhaled a few deep breaths of oxygen, the coughing subsided, and her mind began to focus on her surroundings once again. She was aware of members of her family approaching and speaking to her. She cleared her throat and tried to concentrate on questions.

"Are you okay, Del?"

"I can't believe you ran into a burning house."

"What were you thinking, Delaney?"

All of her sisters hovered around the back of the ambulance. They hugged her and scolded her, and then hugged her again and again.

"Miss Sutton." The parents of the little boy were rushing toward them as Delaney looked over Cassie's shoulder. Jerry was in his mother's arms, still clutching the worn stuffed rabbit.

"Miss Sutton, how can we ever thank you?"

The man held out his right hand to her. "We are so grateful to you for saving our son." He smiled. "We're Jay and Lynda Edwards, by the way, from Alexandria. We came down here for the week on vacation. I guess we could have done without this little bit of excitement. We thank you so much."

Delaney shook his hand. "I'm glad I could help out."

The tall man with streaks of dirt running down his pale cheeks patted the little boy's head. "This is Jerry."

Delaney smiled as the child looked at her and continued to hug the ragged toy. "Hi, Jerry. I'm happy to see that you and your rabbit are okay. What's his name?"

"His name is Hobbit." The little boy grinned. "I went back upstairs to get him."

The child's mother squeezed him until he began to squirm. "Jerry was supposed to be out on the deck playing. We told him to stay there."

Jerry nodded. "I thought I was in trouble, so that's why I didn't answer Dad when he called for me. I didn't know there was a fire, not until you came, Della Annie."

Delaney reached out and smoothed the little boy's blond hair. "My name is Delaney. I understand that you were afraid. It's okay. I'm so glad that you and your parents are all safe now."

Cassie slipped her arm around Delaney's shoulders. "Della Annie is our little sister, and we all think she's kind of special, Jerry. She likes helping people, just like she helped you. I'm sure she'd enjoy spending time getting to know you better. Why don't you and your mom and dad come over to our house? We'll have something cold to drink and visit while the firefighters finish up at your house."

"Oh, that's a wonderful idea." Allison smiled and ushered the three members of the Edwards family toward the Sutton house.

"Come on, Delaney." Brianna hooked her elbow with hers. "Are you feeling well enough to walk back now?"

"Wait, please."

Delaney heard the familiar quiet voice and felt her heart flutter. She looked up to see a firefighter approaching the rescue vehicle on which she sat.

"Gareth!" Cassie rushed up to him. "Is the fire out? Is everything okay?"

He had removed his helmet, and his thick hair was matted to his head. With one hand, he brushed dark stains from his forehead.

Delaney lifted her eyes to meet his, and her breath caught in her throat. The smile that brightened his expression was warm and friendly. His handsome face was smeared with soot, grime, and perspiration, but she still had to fight the almost-irresistible urge to reach out and hug him.

"It appears that there was a short in the wiring that sparked a fire in a kitchen wall. Fortunately, we were able to put it out before it caused much damage."

"That's wonderful news." Brianna smiled. "Cassie and I were getting ready to take Delaney back to the house."

He continued to look at Delaney. "Yes, I was wondering if I might speak with you for a few moments before you headed home."

"Of course, of course—take all the time you need." Cassie did not give Delaney a chance to answer. She took Brianna's hand and pulled her away from the tailgate of the emergency vehicle. "We'll wait over here."

Gareth reached out and lifted Delaney's hands from her lap. "I hope you're feeling better."

She laughed. "I'm fine, but I must look awful. I'm so sooty and dirty."

"You look just perfect to me." His voice was low and husky as he held her gaze. "The Edwards family and most of the people around here consider you a hero."

She felt heat rise up on her cheeks, and she inhaled a deep breath of moist, sea air. "I happened to be nearby. That's all."

"What you did was wonderful, Delaney. You had no idea how bad the fire was when you ran into the house. You searched for that little boy without knowing what you would find. That took a lot of courage."

"I'm a firefighter, Gareth. I know what to do."

"But you've been having doubts."

"I guess instinct and good training took over."

He nodded. "Did you experience any dizziness inside?"

"I did, a little. My stomach twisted and my head spun, but I pushed through it."

"And you're okay now?"

She nodded. "I'm fine."

He squeezed her hands and then set them in her lap. "I'm so relieved that you're all right. When the truck pulled up, I didn't see you standing with your family. I was worried sick about you." He touched her chin with his fingertips. Leaning down, he brushed his mouth across hers. "I know I need a long, hot shower and some clean clothes, but first I need to hold you for just a moment." Without waiting for her to reply, he wrapped his arms around her and pulled her toward him. He pressed his lips against her temple and then nuzzled his face in her hair. "I'm so glad you're safe, Delaney."

His gentle words tugged on her heart as she felt his arms around her. His damp hair rubbed her cheek, and the sensation made her tremble.

"Things went okay inside there for you, even when you had to climb to the upper floor. Does that mean you've come to a decision about your career?"

Delaney swallowed. Uh-oh, there it was. Was he going to try to convince her not to return to firefighting?

She cleared her throat. "I guess it does."

"And what have you decided?"

"I think I've cleared up some of my nagging doubts. I know who I am and what I was meant to do with my life. Getting hurt and then accepting Hal's death were tough experiences for me to get through, but I think I'm better now and ready to do what I've been trained to do."

"So you'll be going back to Richmond?"

Yes, I'll be going back to my life, back to my job. "I can't stay on vacation forever."

"No, I suppose not." He grinned at her. "It was a foolish thing you did, you know. Going into building full of smoke without proper gear or breathing apparatus was reckless behavior, but we're all really proud of you anyway."

His words made her heart race. She wished there was more time—more time to think about their relationship, more time to talk to him about where they were going. At that moment, she was not sure she wanted to imagine a future without the kind, friendly, and attractive man whose smiling face filled her dreams at night.

"I wish you didn't have to go so soon." His comment echoed her thoughts.

"I'll be leaving in less than a week."

He lifted one hand and brushed his knuckles across her cheek. "I wish we had more time to spend together."

Me too. Why did everything have to be so complicated?

"Hey, are you all set, Del?" Cassie and Brianna approached the emergency vehicle as Delaney slid from the tailgate.

She nodded, not trusting herself to speak. She refused to allow her eyes to meet his because she was afraid of the way he could hold onto her without even touching her, but she felt his gaze on her even as she walked arm-in-arm with her sisters, back to the Sutton beach house.

Chapter Eleven

"**I** wish you didn't have to go back."

"Are you sure you can't stay longer?"

"Why don't you call your boss and see if you can get another couple of days off?"

Delaney poured herself a cup of black coffee and accepted the plate of sweet rolls from Allison. The four Sutton sisters were sitting around the balcony off the beach house kitchen as they prepared to eat their last breakfast together before they returned to their separate homes and their separate lives until the next summer sojourn when they gathered again on Hatteras Island.

"I have to go back to work next week, Del." Cassie reached over the space between their chairs and squeezed her arm. "We could drive back together on Saturday."

"Dad and Mom are going to Richmond to see Great

212

Aunt Gen next weekend to celebrate her ninetieth birth-day." Brianna poured Delaney a glass of apple juice. "Couldn't you wait and go back with them?"

Allison smiled at her from across the table as Delaney caught her oldest sister's eyes. "Now, we all knew that our wonderful vacation here would eventually come to an end, as it always does. It just happens that Delaney is the first one to have to leave this year."

Brianna buttered a roll and then wiped her eyes with the back of her hand. "She's always the first one to go." She turned toward Delaney and sighed. "I wish you could stay longer. Why do you always have to rush back to work? I thought you were going to quit your job."

"I've done a tremendous amount of thinking about my career during the past few days. I've certainly had a lot of doubts since the fire that killed Hal, but I believe I've come to a decision about staying on as a firefighter. I honestly can't imagine myself doing anything else." She could not envision her life without being involved in firefighting. The trouble was that she also couldn't imagine her future without Gareth Collins. Her chest felt tight as she realized that she didn't know if she'd ever see him again.

Cassie squeezed her arm again. "And what about Gareth? You've barely gotten together this past week. Have you seen each other at all?"

Delaney tried to ignore the sudden constriction of her heart when Cassie's question verbalized her thoughts. After a long, steady breath, she shrugged as she smoothed the soft fur over Max's back. "We've both been busy with family things, I guess."

She tried to dismiss the feeling of hopelessness flooding her whole body, but it refused to leave. The truth was that she had talked with Gareth a grand total of two times since the fire at the Edwards family's rental house almost a week ago. Both meetings had occurred at Sutton gatherings with lots to do, many distractions, and very little privacy. She had been unable to bring up any subject without the prying ears of one of her sisters overhearing. Conversations with him had been casual and friendly. She still didn't know how her career fit into a relationship with him, and she wasn't sure what feelings, if any, he had for her.

"He's coming over to say good-bye, isn't he?"

"He has to come." Brianna's bottom lip pouted. "You two were supposed to be dating by now."

"And you were supposed to be engaged by Christmas, Del."

Allison handed Delaney a bowl of blueberries. "You seem a little distant from him. Have you two spoken since the beach cookout two nights ago?"

"No, but I'm not distant." She shook her head. "Maybe you can all agree now: Gareth and I have nothing in common."

"That doesn't mean that you don't care about each other. Some couples learn to like what their partner likes." Brianna spooned blueberries from the bowl Delaney passed her. "They discover common interests as they get to know each other."

"Gareth and I are not a couple, and we're not partners. We're just two people who had a few good times on Hatteras Island."

She watched the three older Sutton sisters exchange glances that she refused to acknowledge. If they insisted on playing out the silly charade that Gareth Collins and she were going to become engaged, then she could not stop them. She was returning to Richmond to get on with her life. Her sisters could do whatever amused them.

"Hey, Sutton, will you hurry up with the chow? We're all starving in here."

Delaney brushed a curl off her forehead as she lifted a lid from the large metal soup kettle on one front burner of the huge firehouse stove. It was her first week back to work and, according to her fellow workers, her turn to prepare dinner. Bob Petersen, who was scheduled to help her, was in the game room finishing up a championship round of table tennis in which he had insisted in participating.

"Yeah, Sutton, get with it, will you?"

"You give the kid a few weeks off, and she forgets her duties."

"Those corn muffins had better taste as good as they smell. I think I'm going to faint from hunger!"

Delaney rolled her eyes as she leaned down to take a large tin of muffins from the oven. What a bunch! She had definitely missed the camaraderie at the firehouse, and the fact that she had assisted at two structure fires and a bomb threat earlier that day gave her confidence that her decision to remain a firefighter had been the right one.

She sighed as she set the muffins on the counter to cool and pushed aside another strand of hair that had come loose from the elastic band at her nape. Yes, she was sure she had made the right decision regarding her career. She just was not sure about her personal life.

She still thought about Gareth Collins day and night. The image of his handsome, tanned face and charming smile flashed across her mind at odd moments while she was awake and during her dreams at night.

"Come on, Sutton! Dinner should have been ready five minutes ago. What's the holdup?"

She set a round plate of melon on the large wooden table and then stirred the simmering chili once again. "I could use a little help out here. I shouldn't have to do everything myself while all of you play in your silly tournament."

"We're not all playing. Most of us are watching. And this championship is serious business. We're practicing for our competition with Engine 7 next week."

"Only a girl would call such an important contest silly. Hey, Captain, we should really reconsider letting Sutton stay here."

Bob Petersen appeared, with a sheepish grin on his face, in the doorway of the kitchen. "I'm sorry, Del. I really didn't plan to take so long, but Conrad's winning. You should go watch."

Holding the spoon in midair, she stared at him. "Go in with that loud crowd in there screaming about starvation? You've got to be kidding."

His grin widened. "I guess you have a point. Maybe later."

She shook her head. Maybe after she cleared the table and washed the dishes and cleaned up the kitchen, she would have time to watch the others whack a tiny ball back and forth over a net across a little table. That was exactly how she wanted to spent the rest of her evening. Yes, she was eager to watch a bunch of grown men playing table tennis instead of thinking about Gareth Collins.

Bob leaned over the stove to look into the pot. "What can I do?"

"Set the table. The bowls and plates are already on the counter. And you can get out the jugs of milk and water from the refrigerator."

She watched him round one end of the table as he set down ceramic bowls at each chair. She shook her head in frustration. "You put down too many place settings, Bob. You'd better count again."

"The captain told me to set an extra one out tonight— something about a guest coming."

Oh great, that was just what she needed! It was

probably someone's wife or girlfriend, or worse, a parent, joining them for dinner. All she had made was a huge kettle of chili and three dozen corn muffins with apple sauce and honey. She hadn't even bothered making a fancy dessert. She had sliced up fresh, ripe cantaloupe and washed a bowl of fresh berries to end the meal. No one ever bothered to tell her anything. In irritation, she rotated the knob to turn off the gas under the chili. Well, the rest of the crew could entertain their guest. She planned to eat without making conversation with anyone.

Bob reached around her to grab the utensils from the counter. "What put you in such a bad mood?"

"Nothing's wrong." Her reply snapped out with more force than she planned. "I'm not in a bad mood." She narrowed her eyes as she caught the mischievous glint in those of her coworker. "I could have used more help preparing dinner, especially when one of you inconsiderate guys invited a guest without even bothering to tell me." She set her hands on her hips as she watched his grin broadened. "I don't find any of this at all amusing. What's so funny, Petersen?"

"It's my fault. I'm sorry."

Delaney continued to stare at her fellow firefighter as a spark of recognition shot up her spine. The sound of the quiet, familiar voice coming from somewhere behind her shocked her senses. She had been thinking so much about Gareth that she was hearing him and imagining that he was in the kitchen at the firehouse.

"I guess I should have called first."

She spun around on her heels and nearly dropped the spoon from her hand as she stared at the tall, handsome man in khaki pants and navy polo shirt standing in the doorway. She tried to say his name, but no sound came from her mouth.

"Hi, Delaney."

She cleared her throat. "Gareth, what are you doing here?"

"Well, he's eating dinner with us, for one thing, if you let him." Bob rushed to Gareth's side and added in an exaggerated whisper, "She's not in a very good mood. Are you sure you want to stay?"

Gareth smiled as he continued to hold Delaney's gaze. "I'd like to try to help her improve that mood if she'll give me the chance."

Bob shrugged. "Go ahead and try. Most women are a big mystery to me, even one like Sutton here who usually fits right in with the guys around the firehouse."

Voices from the next room approached, and Delaney inhaled a deep breath. She was aware of fellow firefighters beginning to file into the kitchen to take seats at the table.

"Hey, Sutton, why didn't you tell us you know such a good table tennis player?"

The captain slapped Gareth on the back. "Too bad you don't work for us, Collins. We could really use a ringer like you in the championships next week."

Bob pulled out a chair and gestured for Gareth to

take a seat. "Yeah, too bad. We'd win that tournament if you could play for us against Engine 7."

"What's the big deal, Del, keeping your boyfriend here a secret while we muddle through every table-tennis championship and lose to a bunch of Neanderthals who hoot and holler at us about our lack of talent for weeks until they get the chance to slaughter us again?"

Still stunned by Gareth's unannounced presence at her workplace, Delaney shook her head as she continued to stare at him. "I didn't even know you played." She turned to Bob. "Believe it or not, the subject of ping pong has never come up with us."

Winking at Gareth, Bob slapped her on the arm. "Well, it can't be much of a relationship then, Sutton. What topic could be more important than table-tennis skills?"

Delaney's head swam with the words and noise of conversation and activity at the firehouse dinner table as Bob pushed her into the chair to Gareth's right. If she had had time to consider the consequences of taking a seat so near to the object of her thoughts ever since she'd left Hatteras Island, she would have rushed to the other end of the table or perhaps chosen to eat in a different room altogether.

She breathed a deep sigh of relief as the members of the evening crew began to pass the chili and corn muffins around the table. The conversation turned to other subjects, and no one seemed to notice how quiet she had become. That is, no one noticed except Gareth, who glanced several times in her direction and smiled. When his arm brushed hers and their fingers touched as they passed serving dishes a few times, she shivered from the contact. The intensity in his gaze made her stomach do somersaults, and she tasted neither spicy chili nor buttery muffins. She was aware only of Gareth, the man who filled her thoughts and dreams, the one whose charming smile she couldn't forget.

The melon slices had been gone for at least a half an hour. Bob finished the berries soon after that, and still the captain and other guys lingered around the table talking and joking with Gareth as though he was a member of the company and had been their close friend for a long time. Delaney did not miss the fact that Gareth, too, fit in with the group as though he belonged there. Anyone watching the scene would most likely assume that he was one of them, a professional firefighter ready to move out on a call at a moment's notice.

That was another thing. Why had they not received a call during the entire dinner? It was inevitable that, as soon as they sat down to eat during five out of the seven evenings in a week, the alarm would sound, and they'd have to leave the meal in the kitchen and rush off to answer an emergency call. It was just her luck that no call came in when she could have used a break from the jovial conversation around the table and the intense gaze of Gareth Collins, but the firehouse alarms remained silent.

Finally she was unable to sit brooding in silence any

longer, and she rose from her chair. As she began to clear dishes from the table, Bob rose too.

"I'll clean up, Sutton. I guess it's only fair since I didn't really do my share earlier with the preparations."

The captain cleared his throat. "Go ahead and take a break, Delaney. Bob and the others will wash the dishes."

Bob chuckled. "We'll give you lovebirds a little privacy."

Delaney rolled her eyes. She felt as though she was an unwilling participant in one of her sisters' infamous matchmaking stunts. She expected to see Allison, Brianna, and Cassie rushing out from behind a piece of furniture at any moment as they all yelled, "Surprise!"

She jumped when she felt someone touch her arm. As she looked down, her eyes met Gareth's ready smile.

"Go in the other room."

"Take some time to talk to the guy."

"He drove all the way up from Hatteras. Give him a few minutes."

Delaney's head swam with the barrage of comments and advice from the men sitting around the table. With hesitancy, she met the gaze of his deep, blue eyes.

His smile widened, and her heartbeat quickened. Why did she find that part of him so wonderful, so irresistible? The seemingly easy way his face lit into an expression of simple joy was fascinating to her and made her experience a similar happiness that she felt all the way to her toes.

He had smiled that way when he saw her that first morning peeking out of her bedroom holding Max and wondering who had awakened her. He had also smiled that same way when he picked her up off the floor as he guessed that she was pretending to be Cinderella at the Sutton sisters' silly party. He'd even had one of those charming smiles as he watched his little nieces running and playing at the beach, but Gareth's smile was not the worst distraction that delectable mouth created in her mind. Delaney sighed. She could not get the feeling of it against hers out of her thoughts. She remembered the sweet warmth of his breath against her cheek. She remembered the way his lips fit perfectly with hers and the way they elicited a sensation of pleasure and delight with their movements. She had definitely missed Gareth Collins.

"Come with me." His voice was soft and close to her ear as his hand wrapped around her elbow. His fingers caressed the skin of her arm and made her tremble.

She swallowed and nodded. Without a word, she moved with him toward the door leading out of the kitchen. She forced herself to breathe, and tried to ignore the hooting and clapping of her fellow firefighters that followed them into the next room.

"Is there a place outside where we could go for a little while?"

At first his question made no sense. Nothing made sense, not Gareth's presence there, not the gentle urging of his hand on her arm, not the way her heart was racing as though she was fighting a blazing fire. She shook her head and swallowed.

"Delaney, do you think it would be okay for us to go outside for some air?"

Air, that was what she needed, fresh air. She cleared her throat and nodded.

He led her through the truck bay, between the ladder truck and the rescue truck, and held open the small door next to the overhead one. The street was quiet with just some light traffic and a few pedestrians. "Do you mind if we walk?"

She shook her head and then realized that he seemed to be waiting for a verbal response from her. "It's all right, I guess, as long as I stay within sight of the firehouse. I have to be able to get back right away if the alarm sounds."

"Of course you do." He smiled down at her again. She really liked that smile and the way his quiet voice made her stomach do a kind of quiver thing when she heard it. What was that about, anyway? She was supposed to be annoyed with him. After all, he hadn't even bothered to say good-bye to her.

She felt Gareth's hand in the middle of her back urging her up the sidewalk to her left. She inhaled a deep breath of hot, humid air and matched his leisurely pace.

"Dinner was delicious. I haven't ever had such good chili."

"It's a bit too spicy for my taste, but the guys like it that way."

"I appreciate the invitation to join all of you."

She wasn't sure if the comment required a reply, so she just continued to walk in silence. She heard him sigh and wondered how long it would take him to bring up the reason he was there to see her.

"We didn't say good-bye."

No, we didn't. Delaney tried to calm her growing irritation.

Gareth knew where she was staying on Hatteras Island. He knew her telephone number. Was he implying that she should have tried to see him before she left for Richmond?

"I'm so sorry I missed you that morning. My mother fell and had to go to the hospital. I was in the emergency room with her until almost noon that day. I couldn't use my cell phone there, and I didn't want to leave Mom alone while I went to find a pay phone."

Delaney stopped on the sidewalk and looked up at him. "She fell? Is she all right?"

He nodded and reached for her hands. "She broke her leg, but she's fine." His traced her knuckles with his fingertips. "I'm so sorry I missed you. When Dad, and Jess, and Nate finally arrived at the hospital, I called the beach house, but you had already left."

"I can't believe my sisters didn't give you my home phone number."

"Oh, they insisted I take it, as a matter of fact." The corners of his delectable mouth curved up into a charming smile. "I just thought it would be a little in-trusive of me to use it since you hadn't given it to me yourself."

She stared at him. "You thought it would be more in-trusive than coming to my work?"

His smile broadened, and his eyes sparkled. "Oh, didn't I mention that this is a professional visit rather than a personal one?"

Delaney did not try to hide her confusion. "What do you mean, it's a 'professional visit'?"

"I came to check on you and to make sure you were doing okay now that you were back to work. I wanted see for myself that you were no longer suffering from dizziness and doubts about your job."

"I'm okay, thanks. I'm sorry you came all the way here for nothing."

He laced his fingers around her left hand and slowed his pace. "It certainly wasn't for nothing, Delaney. I didn't get a chance to say good-bye to you, and I haven't been able to think of anything else." As he looked down at her, his blue eyes darkened and locked with hers. "I wanted to see you for myself."

She moistened her lips with the tip of her tongue. "Well, now you've seen me. I'm just fine. You can even report to my sisters that I'm doing all right. No one needs to worry."

He lifted his brows above wide eyes. "Your sisters didn't ask me to check on you."

"Yeah, right, sure they didn't." She intended to make her voice sound light and casual, but she croaked out the words in a hoarse, unfamiliar voice.

"No, I'm serious." He squeezed her hand and stopped walking. "Not a single one of them mentioned me calling her back to let her know how things went tonight."

Delaney ignored her racing heart. She could not allow her growing attraction for the irresistible man standing so closely to her to distract her. She inhaled a long breath. "What exactly are you doing here, Gareth? If you came to try to talk me into quitting my job as a firefighter, you're wasting your time."

His brows lifted higher as his eyes widened. "Talk you into quitting? What makes you think that?"

She took a step from him as his fresh scent of soap and shampoo began to take control of her and make her want to move into his wonderful arms instead of facing the issue of their relationship with a rational mind. "Listen, Gareth. I like you. I like you a lot. Aren't you here to tell me you think I made the wrong decision?"

He gazed down at her for a long moment before he moved his hands to her shoulders. "So that's what this is about? You think I want you to quit your job?" He sighed. "Yes, firefighting is dangerous. As a volunteer, I know the perils of it, the ones you have to face every day. On the other hand, it is the career you have chosen.

You train with serious commitment to keeping yourself and others from harm. You face the dangers of your job in spite of the effects they have on you mentally, physically, and emotionally, because you believe that you're doing good." He smiled down at her. "And you are."

He slid his hands to the back of her neck just below where she had pulled her hair up with an elastic band. His gentle fingers massaged the sensitive skin there and sent a series of tingles down her spine. "Would I prefer to see someone I care deeply about in a less-dangerous profession? Of course I would. Would I like to know that you're not putting yourself in danger every time you answer a fire call? Yes, but I know how much this firefighting career means to you, Delaney. It's a part of you."

He urged her toward him until she was leaning against his chest. "I came tonight to see how you were doing since you returned from your vacation, but I also wanted to see where you work. I wanted to see what makes you get up and come back here every day. I needed to see what fuels the passion of the youngest Sutton."

She looked up into to his eyes to see the teasing there, but she saw only sincerity and an emotion she could not identify. She moistened her lips again. "You needed to see my passion?"

A grin tugged at the corners of his mouth. "I'm speaking of your professional passion, of course, although there is another kind I wouldn't mind learning more about also."

Delaney's stomach did a little somersault, but she tried to focus on the topic of her job. "So you didn't come to talk me out of my decision to stay?"

His mouth was near her ear as he nuzzled his chin in her hair. "No, but to be honest, I did have another reason for coming to see you tonight."

She held her breath. *Now what?*

"I really came to ask you to go to dinner with me some night this week, if you're free."

"This week?" His words were making no sense to her as her heart thumped against her chest.

"I had to drive up for an emergency meeting on a particular case tomorrow, and I'll be here in Richmond doing some follow-up work until the end of the week. I was hoping you had a free night so we could go out to eat and maybe see a movie."

She lifted her head and tipped it back until she made eye contact with him. "That sounds like a date."

"Well, I guess it is, a real one this time, not one planned and paid for by a group of judges for a fundraising event."

She held her breath. "I'm a professional firefighter."

He brushed his fingers along her cheek. "Yes, I know."

"And you still want to go out on a date with me?"

His deep blue eyes darkened, and then he leaned to kiss her temple. "I've been dreaming about it, dreaming about you and spending time with you. In fact, I would like to consider this upcoming date as the first of many, Delaney."

She swallowed as Gareth leaned down again. With whisper soft lips, he caressed her cheek, the one that still tingled from the touch of his fingertips.

Inhaling a long, calming breath, she took two steps back from him and set her palms against his firm chest to steady herself. "So let me get this straight. You don't disapprove of my work?"

His eyes held her gaze. "What is all this about? Professional firefighting is your career. It's a part of you. Why would I want to change that? When I fell in love with you—"

"You what?"

He nodded as a smile tugged at the corners of his irresistible mouth. "I love you, all of you, not just some of you, but the whole Delaney Sutton package. I love the smile in your eyes and the way your hair is always waving in every direction. I love how you let your sisters talk you into doing crazy things and then how you can end up laughing at yourself afterwards. I love that your best friend in the whole world is a temperamental tabby. I love that you love your family and that they come before anything else in your life." He reached up and grasped her hands. "I love you, Delaney Sutton. I just hope that, someday, you can feel the same about me."

A rush of contentment and anticipation flooded her senses. She rose on her tiptoes to kiss his lips. "I already do, Gareth. I love you right now."

Epilogue

Five Months Later

"I still don't understand why we're spending time decorating another tree."

Gareth held one of the multi-colored bulbs up to Delaney, who was perched on the third step of a stool in the living room of his bungalow on Hatteras Island. Her heart jumped as a smile lit up his face and a chuckle erupted from somewhere deep inside him.

"My parents have one. Nate and Jess have one. Your family has one on every floor of their beach house, and we left artificial ones in each of our apartments in Richmond. Do we really need another one here?"

She widened her eyes at him. "This place needed a little festive decoration, don't you think?" She leaned up and to the left to hook the bulb on a top branch of the freshly cut evergreen they had bought at a tree farm

231

in Virginia before driving together to the Outer Banks earlier that afternoon. "There, I think it's just perfect."

He reached for her hand and helped her descend with steady steps to the floor. "Now, can we sit for a few minutes?"

She glanced at her wristwatch. "We still have time to attach a garland to the eaves and then string twinkling lights. I'll go get your stepladder. The party doesn't start for another hour."

He sighed and urged her toward the sofa. "I had something else in mind."

Her heart fluttered as he took a seat next to Max. "We should change for the party."

He patted the cushion on the other side of him. "I'm afraid to ask what the theme of this Sutton family gathering is."

"Theme?" She smiled and gave into his urging to sit. "It's Christmas Eve. That's the theme."

"Are you telling me there'll be no colorful costumes, no interesting games?" He slipped his arm around her shoulders.

"Well, there are the green felt tunics we put on."

His fingers rubbed her upper arm as Max looked up at them and yawned. "And what else is there?"

"Well, we decorate each other like Christmas trees."

Gareth groaned before kissing her neck. "And what about the games you play?"

Her pulse raced as she cleared her throat. "They're perfectly harmless ones."

His lips trailed kisses along her jaw. "I doubt that. Tell me about them."

"We have to guess what's in a disguised gift. Everyone has one specially wrapped by my mother. Then we have to wait until tomorrow morning to open it and find out if we were right."

"That doesn't sound so bad. And what other games do you play?"

"We play charades with Christmas song titles."

"Okay, maybe the games are harmless."

He kissed the corner of her mouth. She trembled and inhaled a deep breath.

"We have props, and everybody pretends not to know the song until at least two props are used."

"What kind of props are they?"

"Like I keep telling you, they're *harmless* ones."

Sighing, he chuckled and set his forehead against her temple. "At least there'll be food."

"Of course there has to be lots of food." She jumped up from the sofa. "Oh, I almost forgot the brownies in the oven. I'd better go check them."

He reached for her hand and urged her back down beside him. "You set the timer. It hasn't gone off yet."

She nodded as she watched him slip a small wrapped box from the pocket of his pants. With a smile, he set it in her palm.

"What's this?"

"It's a present, one of my presents to you. I want you to open this one now."

"It's not Christmas yet."

"It's Christmas Eve." He kissed her cheek. "And I can't wait."

Her fingers trembled as she pulled the tiny red bow from the gold paper and then tore off the single piece of tape. "It's going to take you much longer to unwrap your presents from me. Allison has always complained that I use too much tape."

She smoothed her finger across the velvet hinged box before lifting the cover. As she opened it, a princess-cut diamond set on a gold band reflected the white lights of the Christmas tree.

"Oh, Gareth, it's beautiful." When she looked up at him, his intense gaze locked with hers.

"Will you marry me, Delaney? I love you more and more each day, and I can't imagine my life without you. I want the youngest Sutton sister to be my wife."

Her heart fluttered as he tipped her chin with his fingers and brushed his lips across hers. Contentment and joy filled her as she returned his kiss. "Yes, Gareth, I'll marry you."

"Will you marry me soon, really soon?"

She nodded. "Just don't be surprised if my sisters have already reserved a place for our reception."

His chuckle filled her ears. As he slipped the ring onto her finger, it caught the sparkle of the twinkling lights. Then he leaned down to kiss her again.